Charles Hensleigh

FIRE & RAIN

second Edition

TATE PUBLISHING
AND ENTERPRISES, LLC

Published by Tate Publishing & Enterprises, LLC
127 E. Trade Center Terrace | Mustang, Oklahoma 73064 USA
1.888.361.9473 | www.tatepublishing.com

Tate Publishing is committed to excellence in the publishing industry. The company reflects the philosophy established by the founders, based on Psalm 68:11,
"The Lord gave the word and great was the company of those who published it."

Book design copyright © 2014 by Tate Publishing, LLC. All rights reserved.
Cover design by Joseph Emnace
Interior design by Jomar Ouano

Published in the United States of America

ISBN: 978-1-63122-168-2
1. Fiction / General
2. Fiction / Action & Adventure
14.03.03

DEDICATION

This novel is dedicated to the most beautiful and wonderful wife a man could ever have, my Stephanie. You've been my editor, my sounding board for ideas for this project and others, and you put up with alot to get me here. There are two words alot of hubands forget to say to their wives and they are Thank You. The other three are I Love You.

PROLOGUE

SEEDS OF FLAME

The last piece put in place. The completion of the plan. That's the thing that makes all the difference when all is said and done. That crucial thing can be anything that pushes you past success or failure. The thing in question here is merely a twig.

Just a twig. One tiny little inconsequential stick of brittle wood added to a pile of others just like it. So harmless and yet, so deadly, given the right touch. All the animals in the trees gathered around to see, for they know that truth as well as any human. Maybe more so.

A pair of hands dusted themselves off and one reached into the pocket of a coat. This hand drew something out. The hand held a small box in it's palm and two fingers removed two stick matches from inside. One hand held the box while the other gripped the tips of the matches and slid the heads down the side.

There came the sinister flitting sound as the match heads ignite and the sulfurous odor was left to carry on the breeze. A terrible sound and a horrible smell on a hot night, when the wind was just right, in the middle of fire season.

The lit matches kissed the twigs and the crackle and snap of the dry wood answered it. They burned starting as embers and grew into a small, budding fire. All the animals knew that they must flee, as the shimmering orange glow spreading over the trees and grounds, signaled the panic mode of survival. The man stood, dusted off the knee of his jeans, and slowly backed away. He stood there a moment, waiting and watching as the fire began to scorch the dry grass and leaves on the ground, and tendrils of fire began to spread out. He turned to head for his car parked back in the shadows.

A lone, accusatory squirrel watched him get in and drive away. His nostrils flared at the drifting smoke. Glimmering flames and deepening fear reflected on the surface of his wide brown eyes. With a fretful chittering, he scrambled down the limb of the oak tree and disappeared into the dark.

CHAPTER 1

PARTING SORROW

Thomas Rain was a big believer in the calm before the storm. He gave a sardonic smile at the thought of that old adage, in the bright hot morning sunlight, and the gentle breeze. No one could suspect that not far from the park was a raging inferno destroying woods by the acre.

He flared his nostrils as he took in the faint scent of burning wood. Imperceptible to most, accept for the seasoned Forest Rangers and county crews that do battle with the monster fires every couple of years.

Rain was a Ranger and he could smell it just fine. Like a hinting wisp of a familiar perfume, worn by a long-gone wife or lover. His smile faded slowly away at that last thought.

He looked over at the bronze statue of an old county worker who helped carve out the first of the caverns here at the park. Underneath his immortal form, with his pick ax held high stood his estranged and soon to be long-gone love, Ellie McCormick.

He watched her strawberry blonde hair blowing in the wind and frowned, wondering where and how they went wrong with each other. Their last meeting involved all of five minutes of love making with five days of arguments. She glanced furtively at him as she stood talking to two State Troopers.

As he watched her being briefed by the staties, his frowning visage took on an expression of saddened longing, Rain's best friend and fellow Forest Ranger, John Tatum studied him with a restrained amusement. He glanced between the two of them for a moment. The Troopers finally left her and Tatum tapped his friend on the shoulder. Rain, broken from his reverie, gave Tatum an irritated stare.

"Go over there," said Tatum, "and talk to her. Don't leave her cold."

Rain looked up at him a moment longer, thinking, and then nodded his head once, resigned to listen to his friend. He picked his way through people making their way up the long concrete walk to the Visitor Center and came to a stop close to her.

They stood there, face to face, unsure where to start. Rain looked at her face, her skin that felt and looked so fair and her barely there sort of freckles that could make her seem either girlish and shy or intoxicatingly sexy. She admired his chizzled granite face, his deep tan and black hair starting to gray at the temples. Neither one said so to the other.

"Hey," she said, starting tentatively." Ready to go, then?"

"Yeah," said Rain, and gave an awkward sort of half smile. "I guess so."

There was the awkwardness. The longer than needed pause in conversation of two people who once talked out loud about their every feeling, who now can barely communicate on any level. Ellie took in a breath and let out a long sigh.

"I don't suppose," she said, "you'll call when you get there. Can you?"

"I can, if you want," he said, not meaning for the words to come out so forceably, but they did anyway. This drew a reproachful stare back from her that he would have given anything not to have seen.

"Well," she said, throwing her hands up in a show of exasperation. "It's up to you, Tom."

Rain knew her excitability was brought to the fore by his unintended attitude, yet he couldn't keep that in mind. "There's no need for the tone."

"What?" asked Ellie. She sighed. "There was no tone." she held up her hands to quell the agitated response Rain had opened his mouth to begin, and she stepped back from him a half step. "Call me if you want," she said, calmer now. "I have to go."

Rain glanced around the parking area. A group of vans caught his attention. A camera crew was getting equipment ready to take with them to the cavern. Their on-camera personality and apparent leader Rodger Porter stared back at him.

Rain locked his eyes with Porter's for just a second, and both men looked away. Rain was drawn by the man's eyes, a cobalt blue and extremely icy, with menace that lurked under a sparkling surface. He forced himself to face her again.

"Yeah," he said. "We'll see." Rain turned to go, and Ellie reached out quickly to grab his hand by two fingers. They looked at each other, lingering there, and tears began to show in her eyes. Rain's dower expression began to soften. She squeezed his hand and turned from him. She began her climb uphill on the ramp with the others.

Rain watched her head off, then edged past the crew and their equipment. He headed for the parking lot where Tatum still stood waiting for him. Porter glanced back over his shoulder at Rain's back as he passed by him. He turned away just an instant before Rain took one more parting glance at Ellie.

Tatum was already behind the wheel and shutting his door when Rain got to the car. Rain got in and they watched the State Trooper car pull out of the space ahead of it. Tatum glanced at his friend and backed out. He shifted into gear and quickly fell in a short distance behind the Troopers.

"Everything okay?" he asked.

"I guess," Rain began tentatively, "everything that needed to be said has been."

Tatum nodded. He followed the patrol car around a curve, onto the exit road for the park, his brow knitted in thought. He took a glance at Rain who was beginning to get that thousand yard stare he got when his emotions are tangled, and he decided to prod his pal cautiously at first.

"I wish you could stay with us," he said.

"Me too."

"California?" he asked. He cocked an eye brow at Rain, prodding for an answer.

"It's where I'm from," said Rain. "Grew up there. Took my training there." Rain stared at him in slight irritation that Tatum either didn't see, or pretended not to. Tatum plunged onward, digging under the soft skin, deeper still.

"Still a long way to go," he offered. "The money can't be that good." Rain began to bite at the inside of his lower lip, fighting the frustration and the urge to part on bad terms with his oldest friend. "You guys should try harder to fix things."

"Drop it, man!" exclaimed Rain. "It's over." Rain stared at Tatum, eye to eye, for the longest time. Finally Tatum's expression softened and Rain relaxed. He realized his right hand was clenched around his open plaid over shirt. He forced himself to ease his grip and smooth out the front of his shirt.

"I only said it," Tatum began, "because you're both my friends."

"I know," replied Rain. "Thanks."

Rain rolled his window down and sniffed at the air. He smiled a bitter sort of smile. He thought back over their years together, how many times they had waged war with the wildfires, side by side risking death from heat exhaustion.

"Smoke on the wind," he said flatly. He knew that as soon as Tatum could drop him at the airport he would be back on duty, in the trenches with the county crews, and he, Rain, would be headed out to the sunny and serene California coastline.

"How can you tell?" he asked, incredulously. He sniffed a couple times himself and then shook his head. "That nose of yours, I swear."

"You always forget," said Rain, "that I'm part Blackfoot."

"Which part?" asked Tatum, with a smirk. Rain grinned sincerely for the first time that morning. His grin faded quickly, however, at the thought of what could happen.

"The part that can tell it's going to get a lot smokier soon."

Tatum nodded his head in agreement. He flipped his hand forward at the state patrol car up ahead. "They should just shut the park down right now," he said. "The fire may turn."

They rounded the final bend of the road and came swiftly upon the guard booth at the entrance to the park. The Troopers stop for a brief word with the guard. Rain peered at the through the windshield.

"Where's our regular guard?" asked Rain.

"I dunno," replied Tatum. "Time for him to be headed home, probably."

"Still," said Rain. "I can't believe they stuck some noob up here to make sure no one else gets in."

Rain craned his neck toward the open window, trying to catch a snipette of conversation between the officers and the guard. "We'll be back to shut you guys down in three hours. No one else goes to the park," was the order from the officer behind the wheel. "You got it," was the guard's reply. Rain sat back in the seat.

"I wish they would stay," said Rain, "I would feel better."

"Yeah,"Tatum replied. "So would I." As they followed the patrol out the main gates they both took note of the rising wisp of smoke that snaked it's way into the oppressively heated sky. Tatum spared a quick glance at Rain as he steered them out onto the road. Rain checked his side mirror and saw the gate arms lowered to block entry to the grounds.

Tatum watched the skies and nudged his friend with an elbow. "I bet you wish you were out there," he said. "Right on the line."

"Yeah," said Rain, "I do."

Tatum nodded his head a couple of times, then looked Rain over for any sign of a mind change taking place. "But," Tatum began, "you gotta get to California."

"Yeah," said Rain flatly. "I do."

As they left it behind, the cavern park was getting into gear for the final tour of the day, and likely the final tour until the threat of fire was past.

Families and young couples, elderly adventurers, and Porter and his camera crew milled at the staging area out in front of the wood and stone main building that housed the visitor center.

Porter stood off to the far corner, talking with his men. They all zipped and unzipped their packs, checking equipment and then rechecking. Excited children emerged from the gift shop with ice creams and sodas. Some of the adults took turns at the restrooms.

One of the other tour guides, a doughy wide-eyed man with a paunch whose looks made him seem to be a bit simple- minded, came up to Ellie as she stood beneath a oak. His name was Joey and he was to assist, being as they were escorting such a large group this time. He cautiously and gently tapped Ellie on the shoulder. "You okay?" he asked. "You know, if you don't want to take them all through with me, I think I can do it myself."

"It's all right," she said, forcing a small smile for him. She wiped her eyes with the back of her wrists. "I'll be fine. Just round 'em up and send them to see the video."

"Okay," said Joey. He gave an appraising stare that made him seem more sad than anything that resembled calculating. "I'll meet you back here in about twenty."

Ellie nodded and drifted away from him. Joey turned to the milling crowd of tourists and Porter's stand offish crew.

"Ladies and gentlemen," he began timidly. "If you could, I ask you to go up top to the amphitheater for a short film introduction to the park." A few people clustered together and made their way toward a set of stone steps that would lead them to the glass encased crows nest that Joey pointed to.

"There's some displays up there that'll show you some of the trail areas you can normally go on after tour, but we won't be doing that, I'm afraid. You can also learn about some local wildlife." He looked back over his shoulder. Ellie was watching from the door of the gift shop. "Come back down in half an hour and we'll start the tour."

Ellie managed to give him a genuine smile and mouthed the words, "Thank you" as Joey continued to point the way up the steps, Joey nodded once, then turned from her to watch Porter and his men drift by. Porter cast his cold fire stare toward Joey then at Ellie and moved on with the others.

CHAPTER 2

ACCELERATION

The forest stood in sharp contrast on opposite sides of a highway peppered with various fire trucks, pick-up mounted water haulers, and other official vehicles of the county crew members.

One side radiated destruction as tall pines and oaks stood ablaze their entire heights like emblems of fire. Sentries for an advancing army of a super heated inferno.

The trees on the other side seemed to shrink back, desperate to cling to their vitality and life while they waited for the inevitable incineration. Men and women of the county fire brigades stood ground before them to battle the oncoming blaze.

It was just as trees upturn their leaves as if crying out for rain when it's near falling, only this time, they tried to hide their green limbs, and gave an air of wilting away.

A whip of fire lashed out at four of the county crew fire fighters as they tried hard to man a hose at full stream. Their high powered water blast created mostly steam, putting out a small patch of fire, that flared back up again instantly.

The fire lashed out again, leaping and rushing forward, igniting another row of dry pines. The hose men scattered backward to avoid getting roasted. Crew chief Doug Bradley slammed his hard hat to the ground.

"This is God damn useless!" he exclaimed. He charged forward, calling out to his guys.

"You guys all right?"

They murmured agreement that they were. Other clusters of fire fighters, their trucks parked way back on the road shoulder, raced franticly to spray the newly ignited section of woods. One of the chief's men, Harley Dugger, strode forward.

"We need the fuckin' dump plane now!" He swore. "Where the hell are they?"

"Got the word," began chief Bradley, "before we nearly got killed. They just left base ten minutes ago." He gave Dugger a grave stare as the man tried to figure time. "It'll be more than a God damn hour."

"Great!" yelled Dugger. "Just great!" He glanced to his left, then did a double take, and started in that direction. "Oh, what in the hell...Chief..."

Bradley lazily turned his head to what was going on now. What fresh hell could possibly have sprung up. A line of traffic was headed straight for them down the highway, being led by a county patrol car, along with the worst thing that anyone in their current situation could see. At the front of the line was a medium sized fuel tanker.

Bradley rubbed hard at his forehead, irritated by their turn of luck, and screamed infrustration, "OH-YOU-HAVE-GOT-TO-BE-SHITTING-ME!"

He ran forward with Dugger, both men waving their arms wildly, to try and halt the approach of the convoy.

"No, no, no!" cried Bradley. "Get that turned around!" He made wide circling motions with his arms to show the man behind the wheel of the cruiser. The deputy only drove on. He rolled his window down to talk.

"You gotta turn around!" Bradley shouted, as he made it up to the car. "Now."

"This is the only way!" Retorted the deputy. "The other evacuation route's burning right now."

"All ready?" Bradley asked, incredulously. He couldn't believe what he had just heard. They were cut off and alone in hell. He turned away, fuming. "God, we need that dumper!"

He glanced quickly around as the wind suddenly picked up. A powerful gust from behind the fire bought with it an ominous rushing roar. Just then, the wall of flaming pines in front of them got engulfed by a larger, more brightly orange, wall of fire driven by the wind.

The firey tsunami rolled and rumbled, charging right for the road and engulfed the fuel tanker. The driver died roasting, covered in flames, his screams of anguish and torment cut off by the sound of the raging inferno.

Bradley, Dugger and the deputy stood clustered together. The deputy broke from them and tried to edge toward the truck, knowing there had to be no way the driver was alive, still he tried.

"Give it up, man," called Dugger. The deputy looked backed over his shoulder as he shielded his face with his other arm. Dugger shook his head. "Ain't no way he's alive. Not after that."

Bradley stepped toward them, his brow nitted in concentration, trying to block out the heat and stare at the truck. They began to hear a WHUMP, WHUMP noise in rapid succession. Bradley noticed then that the tank sides had begun to bubble, the thin sheets of steel about to give way from the gas boiling inside.

"Everybody get down!" cried Bradley. He waved for confused firefighters rushing to them with hoses to hit the deck.

"Get down!" He bellowed, "It's gonna blow!" He grabbed Dugger and the deputy by their wrists and dragged them over to the ditch on the far side of the road, shoving them roughly down and landing on top of them.

Just then, the tanker truck exploded, bright yellow and blueish flame erupting into a deadly cloud of ignited gasoline. The force lifted the truck high into the air and deposited the blackened wreck into the field across the highway.

The flames from the gas joined with the oncoming fire and raced over the highway. The field was instantly set ablaze and the torrential firestorm began to reach for more forest at the end of the field.

What was barely contained had now escalated to totally out of hand. Bradley wiped sweat from his eyes with the back of his sleeved forearm and thought there was no way to stop it now.

He looked on at how fast the fire was spreading and knew that he had to get his people out of harms way first. The rest would have to wait a moment.

He looked at the wall of the fire over the highway where the tanker had been and knew that those driving the few cars behind it were gone as well. Dugger and the deputy had gotten to their feet. A woman from the county brigade, came up to Bradley and shared a look of hopelessness.

"Tell everybody to pull back," he said. She nodded and went to do so.

"You gonna call it in?" she asked, "or do you want me to?"

"I'll call" he sighed. "I just hope somebody is even able to help." She nodded and went off to tell the others the plan. Bradley stripped off his gloves, slapped his hands on the legs of his pants to dust them off, and headed swiftly to his truck.

Rain was watching the sky on the distant horizon darken to a storm cloud shade of blackish gray from all the smoke. He couldn't help but frown a little, lost in thought, the uncertainty of what would await him where he was going starting to mount.

He was fighting with memories of time spent around Tatum and with Ellie, some good and some bad, trying to decide what he truly wanted from his life. He had come to the realization that he didn't know for sure.

He thought of bringing this quandary up to Tatum, and had opened his mouth to do so, when the gas tanker explosion lit the distant landscape in a brilliant and blinding flash.

Both Tatum and Rain nearly jumped out of their skins. The explosion was so strong that the shock wave traveled for miles and buffeted their car.

"Holy shit!" Tatum swore. Rain pressed a hand to the dash and held on. Tatum quickly maneuvered the car to the side of the highway. "What in the name of Jesus Christ just happened?"

"I don't know," replied Rain. "County crews bound to be in trouble."

"Yeah," Tatum drawled, miserable. "If they weren't before, they sure are now."

The radio on the dashboard crackled with static. Tatum reached out and tuned it to clear the channel. The voice of Chief Bradley cut through in a panic.

"We've just had a fuel truck explosion out on County Road 79!" he stated emphatically. "We need immediate help out here!"

Tatum tapped Rain hard on the side of the arm. "Fuel truck!" he practically swore. "God!"

"If anyone can hear this," the chief continued. "If anybody can respond to our call, please help!"

Bradley's voice continued on about a new staging ground to battle the energized wildfire. Rain scowled intensely as they listened and shot a look of concern at Tatum.

"The park's cut off," he said. "If that fire jumped the road they have less time."

"What do you want to do?" asked Tatum. He stared intently at Rain, hanging on for what options he may have to offer.

"Go on ahead," he said, "before you get trapped back here too. Tatum opened his mouth to object. Rain cut him off with a determined glare. The very cut of his shark like eyes suggested there would be no begging off on Tatum's part. "Try to help however you can."

"I doubt I can do much on my own," offered Tatum, "but I'll try. What are you gonna do?"

Rain slung the door open and got out. He slammed the door shut and leaned in through the open window. "I'm going back on foot," said Rain.

Tatum looked up ahead, teeth gritted, then turned back to Rain, a worried look to him. "You sure?" he asked.

"Yeah," said Rain, "Go!"

He tapped Tatum on the arm and turned away before more could be said. He ran down from the shoulder, following the tree line back toward the park. Tatum watched him in the rear view mirror for a moment and drove away.

CHAPTER 3

SECURING PIECES

Porter checked his watch. He was on pins and needles, while all around him, the tourists and their children were enjoying the cavern video. The narrator was waxing on about how the stalactites and stalagmites were formed over the centuries.

Porter forced himself to look at the image on the screen. He never cared for science. Found it quite useless in his line of work. He was more a geography man, of a sort. More the explorer type.

He got up from his seat to join two of his men, Rogers and Baker, as they left the screening area. A vision of a bat hanging from the cave walls took up the screen, drawing squeals from a little girl and boy nearest him.

Porter started flinching a little, and gave them a quick sideways cut of the eyes. He was catching up to his men and the drone of the narrator followed him, saying, "Bats frequently inhabit the caves. You may run into them as you go through on your tour..."

Porter and his men navigated around two elderly couples and passed by a labyrinth of wall depicting the early peoples of the region seeking shelter under cliffs, pictures telling the story of the cavern park's first excavators, and various displays of animal life within the walls.

They went to a glass encased model map of the flood plain and river and how it flows through the park by going under the caves themselves. A young native American man in his early twenties, Johnny Two Feathers, stood there in front of it. Porter went up to him.

"How's it going, Johnny?" he asked, startling him. Porter chuckled under his breath. "What do you think? Where's our pretty-pretty?"

"It should be here." said Two Feathers, and pointed to a spot the river flows under a massive section of the caverns.

"I hope," began Porter icily, "for your sake that it is. We've paid you a lot to find it."

Two Feathers whipped his head around, eyes glinting, his temper on the rise. He forced himself to calm down after a dower warning glare from Porter and the one step advance of Rogers and Baker. He smirked at Porter just a little.

"We'll see," said Two Feathers.

Porter had leaned in close to Two Feathers to menace him some more, but was cut short by the appearance of

Joey from around a corner. Rogers and Baker stepped away from them and continued feigning interest in the other side of the display wall.

The video had ended and the crowd was starting to gather. Porter pretended to finish checking out the display, but locked eyes with Two Feathers. "Don't be a wise-ass," he said, and joined the crowd.

"Time to go everybody," said Joey cheerfully. "Hope you enjoyed the video!" He waited for Rogers and Baker to fall in with the rest. Two Feathers took his spot at the rear. "Now, if you'll just follow me..."

They took their positions at the rear of the murmuring crowd. They shuffled and stepped their way, filing out the double wooden doors, that led onto the upper patio area.

Porter grabbed Joey by the elbow as they headed for the stairs, gentle enough to not draw a stare back, but firmly enough to let him know that he meant to deal with him.

"I wonder," Porter began, "would it be possible to have a few words with her before we go into the caves."

He indicated Ellie with a finger point and continued his query. "I want to make sure my men have room for their work."

Joey looked to Ellie. She was standing by one of the great majestic oak trees that populate the park grounds. She was talking to two children.

Porter got a sour look on his face when he noticed they were the two squealers from the amphitheater that had the unmitigated gall to startle him.

Joey glanced up at Porter, meaning to meet his icy gaze, and just decided to nod instead of keeping up the eye contact. Something about the man was just troubling to him beyond anything he had ever known.

"Oh, yeah." Joey said weakly. "Sure you can. Follow me." He proceeded to lead Porter as quickly as he could, wanting to be done with the man, side stepping past the slower moving crowd with him. They came off the stairs and strode up to where Ellie waited with the kids.

"Ellie." He said gently. She turned to him, eyebrows raised. He gestured to Porter before continuing. "This gentlemen would like a word."

"Certainly," she said. "Thank you, Joey." He smiled warmly and drifted away.

"You're Roger Porter, right?" They shook hands. Ellie was brisk because contact with him felt too smooth and snakelike. She had to fight the urge to rub her palm on her uniform pants.

"Yes, I am," he said, and smiled in away that to him seemed to fein warmth. It only made Ellie want to flee in the other direction. She tried to master herself and forced a smile in return.

"And you're with National Geographic, to do a documentary?" she asked.

"Yes. About that-I just want to make sure my men have the freedom to float about and do what they have to do."

Ellie shook her head. "We have to move quickly," she said, "due to the approaching fire. This is the last tour before we shut down, so they need to keep up,"

"I'm sure they will," said Porter. "I can promise they will be..."

One of the kids, Sue, the little girl ran up to them and interrupted. Porter's smile fell as he took a half step back from her. She paid him no mind and spoke directly to Ellie.

"But will we make it before the fire comes?" She asked, her eyes wide with panic. "Are we safe?"

Porter glared at the child. Ellie gave him a reproachful glance and he cut the look short. She bent down to talk to the girl at her level.

"We're completely safe," said Ellie. "I'm sure we are." Ellie looked to Porter again. She gave him a look suggesting that he help in comforting her. He snapped out of his sullen state instantly, the scowl replaced with a cold smile.

"Sure we're safe, sweetheart." he said. "No worries." He turned back to Ellie, wanting to finish their conversation, now that he had placated the petulant girl. "As I was saying..." She cut him off.

"You and your men," she began, "will be given every courtesy. Just as long as you get what you need in an orderly fashion."

She was staring him in the eye. If there was one thing he hated more than anything else was when people made eye contact and tried to keep it. He was unflapped, however, and continued to to smile in his cold way.

"They know what to look for."

Ellie nodded curtly. She stepped away before he could have time to continue their discussion. She turned to face the rest of the group. She had a tour to conduct.

Porter glanced around and noticed two more guides in the souvenir shop. He bit at his lower lip in frustration. There were supposed to be only the two with them on duty.

That's the way of work like this. Nothing ever goes exactly to plan. That's the price for the thrill. The price he loved more than anything to pay. Sill, the unexpected and unplanned for, bites.

"Now, ladies and gents," she began, "gather round. Lets begin the cavern tour! Yeh!"

The kids cheered together. Some pleasant sounds and remarks of agreement came from the group as they lined up two by two along the walkway until all stood at the ready.

"If you'll follow me," said Ellie. "We'll make our way to the entrance point."

Porter drifted back to the end of the line to talk with two of his men, Bowers and Kenner. He pointed back toward the gift shop with a jerk of his thumb. The men cocked their heads that way to look.

"Hang back," said Porter "When we're all inside, go back and deal with them."

Bowers glanced back the way they came. He could see the two guides milling about inside. He smiled.

"You got it," he said.

"Yeah," said Kenner.

Porter started to drift away. He made a motion with his hand by his side for Kenner to come closer. Kenner looked around at the rest of the group and saw no one paying attention to them. He edged up next to Porter.

"Call Eddie up from the gate," he said. "Now that those state bears are gone, he can leave the booth."

Kenner nodded his head. He made another check of the group and tapped Bowers. They hung back staying out of sight, and Kenner took out his cell phone.

Porter caught up with Ellie and Joey at the head of the line, ignoring indignant stares from the other tourists for breaking the line. Ellie stopped at the top of a small flight of stone stairs.

"Okay," she said. "We're about to go inside." She pointed around to some of the tourists. "I see some of you with light coats or extra shirts. That's a good idea."

She pointed out a thermometer stuck to a tree just above her head. Everyone looked in that direction. She looked down at Sue and brother Robbie and smiled before continuing on

"It's about 96 degrees right now," she stated. "Where we're going, the deepest part of the caverns is 72 feet below us, and it stays a constant 65 degrees all year long."

The crowd murmured among themselves Robbie was the first one of them to actually say anything about the numbers given.

"Wow," said Robbie. "That's almost a 30 degree drop." Ellie smiled slighty again as she listened to them talk to each other but she remained focused on the entire group.

"So," she concluded, "wrap up if you need to. Please watch your step and follow us."

Everybody began to form rows and fall in behind Ellie. Joey politely stopped Porter as the tourists passed by them and went inside. Porter held up his hand to halt his men. They all stopped and stood looking on.

"What does the simpleton want now?" thought Porter. He couldn't believe he actually had the nerve to touch him. Most feared him too much to even dare.

"I'm supposed to stay with you guys when we get in," said Joey. "To make sure you're okay."

Porter smoothed out his jacket and his shirt front, letting the man's false bravado fail rapidly, and letting him squirm. He finally looked at him and smiled.

"That's fine with me," said Porter.

They entered the cave then. Porter followed Joey in, with a quick glance back at Bowers and Kenner. They were headed back toward the visitor center gift shop. Porter pulled the door closed.

Rain chugged to a stop before he rounded the bend and the stand of trees that blocked sight of the guard kiosk from the road. He touched at the nape of his neck and felt the stiff and tingling hairs standing on end.

Something was telling him to hide. He crouched down and moved closer, into some tall grass, at the edge of the woods. He watched as Eddie took off his guard uniform shirt and tossed it back into the building and hopped on a golf cart parked beside it.

Rain started. He shrunk back into the trees, as the cart made a turn around and headed up the road toward the park. Rain broke from cover and moved forward at a run, bent low, watching through the trees to make sure Eddie doesn't spot him by a fluke.

He didn't think the man on the cart could spot him now. He was over a small hill and out of sight by the time he had cleared half the distance to the guard station.

That weird prickle of hairs continued. Rain's radar for trouble was switched on and the signal was loud and clear. He wasn't sure what he would find when he reached the station and checked inside, but he knew it wasn't going to be anything good.

Rain reached the guard station and pressed his back against the wall. He breathed deep and tried to steady himself. He fought to slow his breathing and to still his hammering heart.

He turned, reached out, and quickly opened the door. His eyes followed a trail of discarded uniform to the body of a dead man, the real guard, lying in blood and in his underclothes.

"Shit," gasped Rain.

He slammed the door shut and glanced around. He couldn't risk just running up the middle of the road. A guard was dead and who knew what was going on at the park. Then he found what he was looking for.

Rain spotted a shortcut trail through the woods. With any luck, he could get there just shortly after the man on the cart. Then he would find out what was happening here. He ran forward, slashing through the brush, and onto the trail at full speed.

The gift shop was finally deserted. Everyone was headed off to the caves for the final tour of the day and all the remaining attendants, Jacob and Andrew had to do was straighten up the aisle, count the register and basically make everything neat and orderly.

Jacob looked up from his inventory booklet and spotted two men walking their way. He shook his head. It was always something. Tourists would forget their asses if they didn't have to sit on them. He was sure of it.

"Hey, Andy," he said mischievously, "Have I ever told you..."

"Yeah– tourists would forget their asses if they didn't have to sit on them."

Jacob waved his hands as Andrew finished his famous quote, like a conductor with the orchestra, and finished with a flourish of his invisible wand.

"Exactly," he said. "These camera crew idiots are worse yet. They're supposed to be professionals for Christ's sake."

"What?" asked Andrew.

"Yeah," said Jacob. "Here's two of them right now."

Andrew tucked away his broom and came to stand by the counter with his partner. Bowers and Kenner entered the shop. Kenner smiled at them. Andrew nodded in return. Bowers went straight to the soda cooler and Jacob kept an eye on him as he pretended to look.

"You guys are missing the tour," he said. Then he smirked as he thought, "Couldn't follow a straight line, huh?" He glanced at Andrew and two shared a look of mild annoyance at the last minute interruption.

"Tour's over," said Kenner. He and Bowers drew pistols from their shouldered bags and opened fire. The guides had no time to register what was happening.

Andrew was hit in the chest and neck, spraying gouts of blood onto the pannelling of the wall as he fell. Jacob was hit in in the chest and head.

He slammed into the back wall, bloodying the calender and then crashed back against the counter, pulling the register onto himself as he fell, and spilled the contents over the floor.

Kenner moved away from the cooler. He cracked open a bottle of Pepsi as he went and tossed a dollar onto Jacob's prone body as he passed by.

Rain was thundering along the trail. His pulse pounded in his head and his breath rattled from his lungs and out his mouth in ragged rasps. His sweat poured as he struggled to move faster, to out run the man he saw on the golf cart.

He stopped running suddenly, nearly pitching onto the ground, as the echo of the gunfire broke the silence. He took in a few quick breaths and continued running hard, the visitor center not far now.

He rounded a thick cluster of pines and leaped onto two boulders using them as steps and came onto the top of a large dome that had a narrow tunnel passing through the center that park visitors could use to go through the rock. He thought it better and quicker to go over.

He traversed the moss covered dome and dropped down on the other side. He glanced up quickly as he went and could see the tops of the thatched roofs the visitor center buildings had.

Rain ran low, across a field of palmetto trees, and up a hill to the edge of the woods. The man on the golf cart, Eddie, had arrived at the building and was talking to the others. Bowers gestured up to the amphitheater room with his gun hand.

Rain watched Bowers go back inside. Eddie took a doorway that led to the upper room. Rain waited to see him in the large windows.

He saw Eddie pass by the glass and checked the position of the other two. He saw nobody and no hint of movement from the gift shop.

Rain ran across the parking lot to the cover of some ivory and shrubs that peppered the hill. He paused at the foot, checked once more, then scrambled upward.

He kept low, half running and half crawling, and stopped behind the line of shrubbery along the sidewalk, just a few feet from the entrance to the shop.

CHAPTER 4

TATUM GETS FIRED UP

Tatum was sweating with the air conditioning on high as he sped down the highway through the fire zone. Scorched earth and blackened trees flanked his sides.

He topped a hill and saw the new encampment of the county crews lay down below. He glanced to the left, down a service road where more firefighters were, a long distance down with fire swarming in the trees all around them.

He drove on, coming upon the heart of the battle and was waved to the roadside by two of the men from the crew. He slowed quickly and wrenched the wheel left maneuvering the big Sedan onto the shoulder.

He got out and the men relaxed when they saw his uniform. They had to be relieved he was a Ranger and not some ninny out to see the show. Tatum went up to one of them.

"Where's Chief Bradley?"

"Over there," said the fireman. He pointed back behind himself to a portly man directing a line of hose wielding crew trying in vain to put out a swelling rush of fire that advanced with the wind.

"Thanks," said Tatum, and clapped the man on the shoulder. He headed that way.

Bradley and his crew rallied. They drifted back and continued to spray the flames from large tankers.

"Don't trip up on that hose!" shouted Bradley.

"Everybody fall back! Keep fighting!" yelled Dugger.

"Yeah, that's it!" yelled Bradley. The wind died down and they quelled the flames with their torrents. The men sagged, letting the heavy hoses drop to the ground. Bradley wiped sweat from his stinging eyes and blinked to clear his vision as Tatum stopped in front of him.

"You chief Bradley?" asked Tatum. He extended his hand and Bradley hesitated, then shook it, nearly forgetting politeness in such a trying time.

"Yeah," said Bradley. "You're the first Forest Ranger we've seen. Where's the rest of your guys?"

"Down at the other end of the county," said Tatum. "I was the only one in the area. I'm John Tatum, by the way."

"Tatum?" asked Bradley. Tatum nodded. "Good to meet'cha."

Bradley led him away from the others and pointed to a deep trench in the ground they had been digging. "I guess you saw some of this on your way in?" Tatum nodded. "We're diggin' as fast as we can. If you want to help out with it, go on down to the end of the line."

Tatum looked over his shoulder at the trench. He could see others in the distance shoveling out more dirt. Their trail led toward the road he saw on the way here.

"That's where I saw the other crew?"

"Yeah. We're trying to surround it. Don't know if we can though."

Tatum watched the fire a moment. He furrowed his brow and bit at his lower lip. He glanced up the hill beyond the road where the other part of the crew labored on the trench.

"It'll slow it down," said Tatum, "but it won't stop it. I'm going to have to set a back fire past your diversion point.

Bradley's smile faded from his face in an instance and an incredulous stare replaced it just as fast. He couldn't believe what he was hearing. All day long the blaze had knocked them back and the gas tanker made it even more difficult to contain. Now this.

"A back fire?" he questioned, his voice cracking with emotional strain.

"That's right," Tatum stated evenly.

"The fuckin' woods are already burnin' faster than we can put 'em out, "he yelled, "and you want to add to it?"

"That's the only way," said Tatum. Bradley just looked at him like he was talking giberish.

"Fire runs up hill. What if it gets around your trench instead of running into it?"

Tatum glanced that way, toward the rise that he drove over when he came to the camp. Bradley followed his gaze, but continued to show disapproval.

The man looked as if some foul smelling funk had taken up residence directly under his nose and there was no way to get rid of it.

"Well, you just do what you gotta do then."

The crew chief practically stuck his nose in the air and turned on his heels to trudge angrily away. The childish gesture would have seemed comical under different circumstances. But not today.

"I will," retorted Tatum. "It's the only way and you know it, Chief!"

Bradley continued to stomp off toward his men and waved a dismissive hand at Tatum. Tatum turned his back and headed for his station wagon.

Tatum took it easy. He was used to driving these state owned trails on a four wheeler, not a big family car, so he drove at a snail's pace.

Tree branches scraped and slashed at the sides of the car, screaming off the metal sides, leaving grooves in the paint job. A thick tree trunk snapped off the left side mirror.

"Aw, shit," said Tatum. He slowed nearly to a stop and crunched his way through between the big trees. The car made it through the gap and he was in a clearer section.

He pulled the car to a stop in a small clearing and got out. He glanced into the sky. The thick smoke from the fire loomed ominously overhead like sinister storm clouds. He checked his direction, waiting for the wind to pick up a bit.

He reached into the back window of the wagon and took out a gun that looked like the sort they use for paint ball warfare, with a wider opening on the barrel.

He stepped away from the car to an area of intensely thick under growth and dry brittle bunches of grass. All this section of trees, from here back to beyond the park was pine, and would burn hot in a short period of time.

The wind whispered to him as it rose in the forest and rushed through the area. He pulled the trigger and sent four golf ball-like incendiary devices into the thicket.

The dry wood and leaves and grass caught fire quickly, flames rising onto trunks of the pines. Tatum quickly fired two more of the golf balls, instantly igniting more of the undergrowth.

The firebreak spread out, and ran uphill at an alarming pace, driven by the swell of the wind. Tatum head back to his vehicle.

CHAPTER 5

RAIN'S SPARES/THE TURNCOAT

Rain felt ready to break. His body was coiled tight as a spring and ready to snap. He waited longer to make sure he saw no further movement from inside.

He poured sweat, his iron muscles about to split his shirt, he was so tensed for the action. His heart thundered and his eyes darted. He bit the tip of his tongue as he concentrated on his objective.

Rain readied himself, rocking back and forth on the balls of his feet, and sprang out darting low and silently across the sidewalk and into the gift shop.

Rain ducked down, crouched almost to the ground, as he edged behind the counter with the bloody bodies of the two guides. He peered over the top of the counter.

Bowers drifted farther away and began flipping through post cards and Kenner crossed to the windows to stare out.

Rain carefully climbed over the bodies and went through the open doorway to the barracks of the park tour guides. He had to be careful not to make a sound, not an intake of breath or scrape of a shoe as he went.

He stood up, deep red from the strain on his body, and sweat rolled off him, dotting his shirt and dripping on the floor around him.

Rain checked behind him, making sure he heard no movement toward his position, then cautiously crept deeper into the barracks. He passed benches and lockers, went behind a wall to a row of lockers at the back wall.

All the lockers had a name plate for the guide that would be on detail for the cave tours. He moved to the left end of this final row and found the brown locker with the name ELLIE McCORMICK on the plate.

He checked the combination lock, giving it's round works a gentle tug. Good old Ellie. She always left her lock undone because she could never remember her combination. Rain smiled as he thought of her placing the lock barely together, just so, to make it appear locked to the naked eye.

He opened the steel door quietly, his teeth clenched in anticipation of a squeal or squeak, but none came. He opened the other side and at the back of the locker was a piece of masking tape. On it were two words printed in capitals in black sharpie marker: RAIN'S SPARES.

Rain's spares were a forest ranger uniform, no weapons, just clothes and belt of gear. He took these out, and after one last glance behind him for trouble, he prepared to change.

Lights flooded the cavern room the tourists were standing in. Gasps of amazement went up from the crowd at the sight of a large, glittering rock formation that appeared to be the largest iced cake in existence.

Ellie came from behind a rock and stood at the front of the group. Two more of Porter's men, Owens and Sully, pretended interest, snapping a few photos and then looking away again as though they were here for something else. Her voice carried in the chamber for all to hear.

"Now," she began, "We're standing inside the wedding room. It's called that because the rock formation directly in front of you looks like a giant grand wedding cake with thick layers of icing."

"Oh," said Sue. "It looks good enough to eat!"

Ellie smiled. Her little brother frowned at her and some laughter came from the tourists.

"Yeah," said Ellie, "but I can assure you it's not very yummy."

People drew in closer to get pictures and admired how the crystals in the rock glitted and twinkled at them like a million points of light.

"The crystals in the rock," continued Ellie," give off light and make it appear to be icing on the cake."

Sue and her brother Robbie moved closer to Ellie, trying to get a better look. She took a picture with her little camera and Robbie cocked his head this way and that, watching the light reflect off the crystals. "Cool," he said. Ellie patted his ball cap covered head and he grinned at her.

"Before we go on," began Ellie, "I have to tell you we actually perform anywhere from seven to ten weddings a year, right here where you stand."

She moved away from the group and went behind the small rock again. She crouched down at the electrical box and prepared to shut off the lights to the formation.

"Okay," she said, "Lights out."

Ellie flipped the red handled switch and the bright beams faded out, leaving only the soft light from overhead. She took her place at the head of the group. "This way, guys," she said, and led the group out of the wedding room to a trail leading them further into the caverns.

Joey ushered Porter and his men to continue moving forward with the others in the tour group. They had huddled together at the back. They needed to keep moving.

"Keep up guys," he said, "That way." He pointed with the butt end of his flash light. Porter smirked around at the men and some chuckled.

"Yeah, sure," said Porter. "No problem." They took a few quick jaunts forward and were again at the back of the line.

Ellie was shining her light on a display of rock that looked like a giant pipe organ where cracked walls of rock met stalactites that dangled from the cave ceiling.

Next to that was a smaller formation of a similar type. Ellie shined her beam all around both formations. Joey gave Porter and his men the sternest look he could muster. Porter whispered to them, smirking, and they drifted away from Joey.

"These pipe organ-like formations are what give the Cathedral Room it's name," stated Ellie. More pictures were snapped and Ellie moved back to the head of the line and turned to the wall.

"Next," she began, "We're going into one of the most stunning rooms in this entire cavern- the Christmas Room." A few of the tourists shared bewildered looks with their fellow companions.

"A harmless gas emanates from the ground in this room," continued Ellie, "and it gives the rock formations, their unusual colors. The colored lights in the ceiling above each one are used to indicate and enhance the color in the rocks."

She started to enter the room and she spoke over her shoulder to the group as they followed carefully behind her. "Some workers are in here to check the gas levels. They do that on occasion, so don't mind them. They..." she stopped.

The tool boxes the workers brought with them were on the cave floor but there was no sign of them. "Where are they?" she asked. She turned to look for her partner. "Joey, do you know where they went?"

"No," said Joey from the back of the group.

At that instant, the sound of drilling came to them, echoing from the distance. The cave floor vibrated under their feet. It was coming from down the ramp at the lowest chamber of the caves, an area usually off limits during rainy seasons, because the underground river tended to flood it.

"What the hell is going on?" asked Ellie.

Joey shrugged. He followed after the group as they all, confused and concerned, followed Ellie. She wound and side stepped her way past close cave walls and started down the ramp way to the lower chamber.

Upon entering, she saw the two men, Cates and Dixon drilling holes into the rock floor. They stopped drilling and stared at her. Ellie looked incredulous. She must have seemed daunting to them for they exchanged worried looks.

"What do you think you're doing?"

The men stood their ground and said nothing as she stepped into the room. The crowd formed a tight circle behind her but kept their distance. A sick fluttering sound of ripping cloth issued from behind them all and they parted as Joey staggered forward into the room, hands clutching his stomach.

Blood squirted from between his fingers. A glimpse of intestines were visible as he entered the light set up for the dig site. Gasps of fright and screams at the initial apperance of him were followed by an immediate stunned silence.

Porter stepped out from behind Joey and came up by his side. The bloody curved blade of his knife gleamed red in the florescent glare. He smirked at Ellie.

"Ellie...Ellie," called Joey, "He...He..."

Porter closed a hand over Joey's mouth and pinched his nostrils closed, suffocating him where he stood. Joey made snuffling noises and twitched in Porter's grasp.

"Shhh...sshhh," Porter whispered. "It's all right. No worries now."

Joey stopped moving and Porter let his prone body crumple to the floor. More screaming and yelling filled the room. Two men helped an elderly lady to the ground after she fainted. Ellie stepped toward Porter, an angry sneer on her lips.

"You son of a bitch!" she yelled. All around, amid the tour group, Porter's other men drew their guns and pointed them at Ellie. She stopped in her tracks as they took aim at her. She looked from them to Porter. "What are you people doing?" Porter glanced up at her. He had dropped to one knee and was using the leg of Joey's pants to wipe the fresh blood from his blade before it began to get sticky.

He stood up, dusted his jeans off, and tucked his knife back in its scabbord. He stepped closer to her, smiling his cold smile as he came.

"As you can probably guess," he began, "we're not from National Geographic and there is no documentary."

Porter's men began pushing the tour group into a tight cluster, training their guns on them. She looked to them and faced Porter again. She suppressed a shiver and tried not to look down at Joey as Porter stepped over his leg and came closer still.

"What do you want?" she asked.

"Gold," he said, as if it were the most logical answer in the world. Ellie raised her eyebrows. "Yes, my dear. Gold."

"You see," he continued as he glanced around the crowd. "I have it on good authority-" He dragged Two-

Feathers into the circle of light with them. "- that a fortune in Seminole Indian gold is hidden in the underground river that flows through this park. We aim to recover it."

"Recover?" asked Ellie, sarcastically. "You mean steal it."

Porter chuckled at her. He kept that cold smile fixed firmly on his face. Ellie fought with herself again and willed away the full body shiver that yearned to run through her. He gestured with a good natured wave of his hand, patronizing and dismissing her.

"Mere semantics," he said.

"Are you going to kill the rest of us?" she asked.

"Not if I don't have to," he said. He pushed Two-Feathers back toward the group. "I'd prefer to keep you all as cover. The fire could turn this way and we may need to be evacuated."

He turned away from her and faced Dixon and Cates. "Keep dirlling," he said. They simply put their heads down and got back to work.

CHAPTER 6

COVER AND CONCEALMENT

Rain's heart thudded in his chest like a jackhammer encased in his body. At time it threatened to rattle his very flesh from the bones. He was unarmed and out manned in a situation that he hand no clue how to handle. He had to try.

He needed to know where Ellie was and if she and her tour group where still alive. If finding out meant he had to test himself in mind, spirit, body and sheer will against an army, then so be it.

Rain had made his way back out of the locker room and past the men in the gift shop, still staring out the windows and keeping watch. But they had left the door open and watching had become useless. Hell was here and it was time to burn.

Rain checked his corner, then crept up the stairwell, keeping his eye on the gift shop. He could still hear Bowers and Kenner moving around. He crawled his way near the top of the stairs, then stopped, pressed flat and listening.

He edged forward, near the landing, where his query waited in the amphitheater. He popped his head up to peer in. Eddie drifted from between two of the display case walls and circled behind another. Rain gnashed his teeth in anticipation of cornering him.

Rain tensed, as if frozen, upon hearing the scuff of shoes on tile from behind him. He glanced back over his right shoulder and could see the shadow of one of the men downstairs. The shadow moved away and Rain continued breathing.

He got to his feet in a crouch and eased himself onto the landing. He stood slowly, willing his knees not to pop and crack, and relaxed himself for a moment. He heard Eddie move and darted to his left just in time to avoid being seen.

Porter prowled the narrow pathways of the caverns, moving from room to room not taking in any sights, but moving for the sake of movement. He was almost like a great white shark, how they had to keep moving or risk death, and that was also true of Porter.

He allowed himself a smile at the thought of it. Roger Porter, the great white shark of the underground river. His twisted half smile broadened and he bared all his teeth, standing there grinning at himself with all his teeth showing.

One of his men entered the chamber where he was and nearly fell back out upon seeing Porter that way. Porter snapped himself out of his fantasy reverie and stalked toward Dillon.

"Yes?" inquired Porter testily, "What is it?"

"They broke through, sir," managed Dillon. He was still far too scared of Porter to look him directly in the eye. So he pointed the way and looked at the ground as Porter shoved his way past.

Porter entered the lower chamber where the dig had been commenced earlier in the morning. Chunks of rock littered the cavern floor. Dixon and Cates were standing over their small crater, looking down. Dixon glanced up at Porter and smiled. Porter could hear the rush of the fast moving river water as it cut it's way underneath the park.

He went over to them. Cates jumped back out of the way to let him have a peek. The water was practically like rapids. The descent of the river was all down hill so it ran swiftly. Cates tapped him on the shoulder.

"Our native friend says the gold's in the river bed."

"Excellent," said Porter. "Then make haste."

Rain was standing in the amphitheater screening room, where the tour group watched the introductory film of the cavern park, not very long ago. He tried to master his breathing and get himself quiet as a whisper through the trees.

He paused at the movie screen taking up the wall behind him. He turned and looked at the message on the screen. The blue letters prompted in flashing capitals: PUSH BUTTON TO RE-START FILM.

Rain glanced up and spotted Eddie's shadow flitting across the wall. He reached out and pushed the button down with the palm of his iron hand. He then moved quickly away to his right.

Eddie was amusing himself, checking out a display wall of plant life found at the cavern park along it's scenic flood plain trails, when the film started up again. He gave a jerk, startled by the voice of the narrator.

"Welcome to the Marietta Caverns state park," it said.

Eddie frowned. He leaned out toward that direction and stared. He listened for movement or voices, but he couldn't hear anything over the volume of the movie. He took a step in that direction.

"Hey, guys...is that you?"

No answer came. He scowled, annoyed that they might be pulling some kind of prank on him. They were always doing that. Always being assholes to him because he was younger than everybody else. They all thought he was a screw up, just a stupid kid. "We'll, I'm almost 25, you dickheads," he thought. He took a couple more steps their way.

"Quit screwin' around," he commanded.

He drew his pistol and held it at his side. He strode toward the screening area. From his left side, fast as a black panther came Rain, launched through the air with arms spread for the tackle.

Eddie tried to whirl and bring the gun up to fire, but Rain was already on him. He caught Eddie's wrist on his gun hand and curled his other arm around his midsection and down on the floor they went.

The gun tumbled off to the side. Rain slammed a beefy forearm into Eddie's nose and mouth, flattening the appendage with a great gush of blood and the squishing noise of pounded cartilage.

Eddie howled in pain and rage. He drove a knee into Rain's side, knocking him off. From below them came the panicked voices of Kenner and Bowers.

"What's going on?" asked Bowers

"I don't know-just shut up!" yelled Kenner. "Eddie, you okay?"

"Get up here!" screamed Eddie.

Rain punched him in the head. Eddie twisted away and grabbed the gun. Rain got to his feet, lighting fast, and ducked behind a display wall just before five rounds from Eddie slammed into it.

Rain had underestimated how wiry and quick Eddie was. He wouldn't make that mistake with anybody else again. Plaster and wood chips sprayed past him as the bullets missed by inches.

He could hear Kenner and Bowers thundering up the stairs now. Rain launched himself into the display wall nearest him with a guttural grunt and heaved it over.

Eddie screamed and tried to cover himself as the heavy wall came crashing down, crushing him under it's bulk and sending the gun clattering away. Rain tried to make a grab for it as the men entered the room. Kenner fired off four quick rounds.

Rain ducked behind another display wall. Bowers took out an AR-15 machine gun from his bag and unleashed a full clip as Rain slung open the back doors and ran across the patio.

Glass windows and wooden framework splintered and shattered, exploding in a hail of debris as Rain ran away, shielding himself with a forearm as he passed out of sight.

"Fuck!" yelled Kenner.

"Let's get him!" cried Bowers.

They jumped through the jagged holes where the full length windows were, giving chase.

Rain grappled with several thoughts that ran through his mind at once like errant juggernauts on a collision course. One crashed and burned against another and others slammed into the last. He tried to form coherent facts in his head as he traversed the uneven and steadily climbing ground.

What was going on here? There was the fire. It was coming fast thanks to the tanker explosion. Now there were people trapped here at the park, down in the caves, with no clue what was happening up above. Why were the armed men here? What was their purpose? The questions had no end.

Rain was vaguely aware of sounds. They all seemed to come to him from far away, almost as if heard through a wall. He heard the crunch of glass as they went through the windows after him. He could hear bits and pieces of their grunts and strained breath as they chased him a short distance behind.

He gritted his teeth and bore down, trying to put every ounce of his body's flagging stamina into the long uphill run of the over look trail. He tried to master his rampaging brain and calm the crashing thoughts until all he heard and felt was his hammering heartbeat.

Rain grunted, breath came fast, as he charged hard along the rugged path, barely more than rocks and tendrils of tree root. He reached one of the tallest points and could see the visitor center far below him.

Bullets punched into the dirt and foliage around him was reduced to frapeyed, dripping bits of green waste as Kenner and Bowers spotted him and opened fire.

Rain lowered his head and willed his legs to move. They felt like thousand pound anchors that threatened to entrench themselves in the dirt and drag him to a halt. Still he plowed ahead.

Rain leaped a fallen log and scrambled up the tiny ridge ahead. The trail curved sharply to the left, but dead ahead was a sudden drop off of a granite cliff face that reached some seventy five feet below.

Two birch trees stood ten feet out, their tops marking the canopy of the plants growing in the chasm. These trees were practically choked with thick vines.

Rain yelled defiantly, a deranged war cry, as he hurled himself out. He grabbed a vine in his iron hands and swung himself around the back side of a mighty birch, slamming into it so hard he nearly lost his breath. He fought the crush of the pain and flattened himself against it carefully, his fingers and the tips of his feet clinging to the ancient bark, the vine still grasped in one meaty arm. He struggled to maintain his grip and not slide off. Finally, he found purchase.

Bowers and Kenner came panting to a stop, hands grasped onto their knees. Bowers checked back the way they came. Kenner stood and searched the other turn of the trail and found no sign of their query. Kenner kicked a rock down the trail.

"He's gone!"

"Gone?" asked Bowers. "How? We were right behind him."

"Do you see anybody?"

Kenner shook his head and threw his hands in an aggravated gesture. Bowers went to the edge of the cliff and tried twice to peer over the side. He saw nothing. No sign of anyone below.

Kenner waited for a response then turned to him to prompt one.

"You see him?" asked Kenner.

"No! No sign at all."

"Where the fuck could he be?" asked Kenner. He spun all around, looked in every direction. Still nothing.

On the tree, Rain listened intently, and continued to hold himself there even as he trembled with the effort. He dared not move the slightest bit for fear of falling or giving himself up.

If he moved and bark fell from the tree, they would hear it and see, then they would open fire and he had two choices at that point – fall to his death or hang here and be killed. He trembled again and wondered how much longer he could hold on. Kenner peered over the edge.

"Okay," said Kenner, "Let's head back. We'll call Porter from there."

Kenner moved away from the edge. Rain mouthed the name of Porter and listened to their footfalls go shuffling back the way they came. He hung on a moment longer. When a tremor came again and didn't stop, he knew he had to move.

Rain eased himself off of the tree and onto the thick grapevine in a rope climbing fashion. He slowly and methodically slid down the length of the vine until he reached a point where it tapered off about ten feet from the ground.

He glanced up at the top of the hill and waited to see if his movements had betrayed him. No faces peered down at his and no gunfire rang out. He let go and dropped to the ground in a crouch. He spared another look up to be sure, then he swiftly moved away. Now he had a name. That was a start. Now, he needed more.

CHAPTER 7

THE FLY IN THE OINTMENT

The hostages were gathered in a large group, bathed in red, blue, green and yellow light of the Christmas Room. The stalactites and stalagmites seemed to stand guard under their different hues.

Porter's men patroled the front and back entrances to the room. Ellie watched them with growing distaste evident on her pinched features. Distaste deepened to near stomach lurching sickness.

Porter had appeared in the doorway. He smiled. His shiny whites glinted in the dark shadows as he stepped inside. He looked around at everyone with a smarmy little grin stretched across his face. The flippant gesture made him seem like nothing more than a party host checking on his guests.

"Are we all comfy?" he inquired. "I trust the accommodations are to your liking."

Nobody answered. No one even gave a murmur or even a glare of dissent. He glanced over his shoulder and smirked at Ellie. She gave a sour stare at him and stretched out her legs from underneath her as he came over to her.

"What are you going to do with us?"

"I'll let you go once I have what I need."

She raised her eyes to him and met his cold gaze. Her questioning eyes prompted him to continue. He could tell she didn't believe a word of what he said. So what if she didn't?

"That is," he said, "If you're all good."

She stared at him in disbelief. "If you give me any trouble, though-you can stay here and burn. The fire is closing in."

He gave her another of his chilling smiles and turned to go. She got to her feet, dusted off her pants, and stood straight and tall with her hands on her hips.

"How exactly are you going to make it out of here with all that gold...if we get evacuated?"

He stopped and turned halfway around to look at her. The corner of his mouth turned up in a hate filled sneer. "I have fire insurance," he began. "Don't you?"

He raised his eyebrows. Ellie frowned at this. She wondered what he meant by his caveat and it must have shown on her face, because Porter laughed. His laugh made her shudder. It was more of a bark and cold as a winter north wind.

"What?" she asked.

Porter started to retort. He snapped his mouth closed in a tight lipped frown as his radio began to beep. He smiled at her and held up a finger as he gripped it and brought it up to talk. He turned away and went out of the chamber out of ear shot of the hostages.

"Yeah?" asked Porter.

His smug grin slowly disappeared as what he was hearing angered him. Ellie couldn't help smiling. She couldn't make out a word of what was being said to him, but it clearly agitated him.

"What the bloody hell do you mean some forest ranger?" he asked. Ellie perked her head up. Listening as Porter turned away. "I thought they left here."

There was mere garbled reply and his shoulders tightened visibly as he put his head down, continuing to listen. Ellie watched and wondered who it could be. Had Rain come back? Was it Tatum? What were they doing back here?

"Well did you get him?" He listened and then clenched his fist. "Oh, fucking great! I'll send you some help. Track him down and kill him!"

He flicked the radio off with one hand. He stormed out of the chamber. Ellie scowled at Porter's back as he went away.

"Looks like I've got fire insurance too," she whispered. Allowing herself a confident smile. Porter stuck his head back in, and she jumped back. He shook his head at her.

"Not for long." he said. Then he was gone.

Ellie crossed her arms over her chest and stepped back over to the group. She sat down and hugged her knees to her chin, her mind racing, as she looked out the chamber entrance. Once more, the guard paced.

"We'll see."

Rain was moving slowly, methodical in nature, as he worked his way along he uneven ground of the floodplain. He broke off from the trail not long after he had dropped from the vine for fear of being tracked.

That would be more difficult to do here. The floodplain was covered with rolling hills and gouges in the land where the violent and swift flood waters cut their pathway through in the rainy season.

Drifts of detritis like crumbling mashes of leaves and twigs lay in thick, hip deep piles in the deepest groves and shifting ground and the waste that covered it hid his footfalls very well.

Still, he managed to move lightly, mostly on the balls of his feet so a heavy full step would not show up in the dirt. If anything, his trail would appear like nothing more than that of the herds of wild boar or the bears and deer that wander the area from time to time.

Rain spotted a large circular bow-like shape in the path ahead. He stopped and eyed the ground all around it with careful, calculating eyes. He smiled slightly and moved to the left. He made his way, cautiously impacting the ground, and stepped in a wide arc.

He stopped still as a large limb, rotted to the core, broke free of an old oak tree and fell to the ground. It hit the circular indention that Rain was circumventing and a mucky brown wave of mud and leaves spread out from around it. The limb began to submerge in the quick mire.

Rain continued on. With any measure of luck he should find what he was looking for in short order.

Two more of Porter's goons, Hedger and Griggs, milled around at the spot where the others had lost Rain not long ago. Two-Feathers paid them no mind. He was looking intently upon the ground and spotted an indention.

Bowers and Kenner were standing close to him. They watched him and their stare burned into him. He could tell they were trying to intimidate him. He looked carefully at the vines and frowned.

Two-Feathers bent suddenly and reached out to grab a large stick on the ground. Kenner kicked him on the arm and turned his gun on him. Two-Feathers stood up and held his injured arm.

"What the hell are you doing, chief?"

"I need that stick," said Two-Feathers. He rubbed at his arm and gave Kenner a stoic once over. Kenner looked down at the stick and smiled at Two-Feathers.

"Gonna carve yourself some arrows or something?"

Two-Feathers ignored his taunt. He turned his head and looked instead to Bowers. Bowers smirked at him, then reached past Kenner to get the stick. He handed it over to Two-Feathers.

Two-Feathers took the stick and reached out over the edge to hook the nearest vine. He got hold of it and pulled it in so he could inspect it. He peered carefully at it for a moment and nodded.

"He went down," said Two-Feathers. He let the vine go and dropped the stick. He eyed Bowers as he wiped his hands off on his jeans. "He's going along the floodplain trail."

Bowers turned to their backup. Griggs was crouched in the dirt handling mushrooms and Hedger watched him with mild curiosity as he was told all about how to make tea out of them.

"Yeah," said Griggs, "Once you drink it, you'll see some shit, man. Crazy shit."

"Hey," said Bowers. Griggs didn't hear. He kept picking the mushrooms. Hedger did a take and stepped back, realizing what Bowers was about to do. Griggs never noticed until the rock that Bowers kicked smacked into the back of his head. He yelped in pain, let go of his crop, and stumbled back up to his feet.

"What the..."

"Pay attention," snapped Bowers. "The chief here says our man went down." He pointed over the edge of the cliff. He surveyed them both and decided Hedger was the most competent, so he talked to him.

"You come with us." He indicated Two-Feathers with tipping his chin toward him. "Your buddy can take him back to Porter."

Two-Feathers watched their exchange with a growing curiosity. He needed to make sure that what ever happened, he didn't go back into the caves. He stepped toward them. "You need me," he said. Bowers raised as eyebrow at him. "There's all sorts of traps out here for him to use."

"Shut your mouth!" snapped Bowers. "Porter wants you where he can lay hands on you... seeing as you're not trustworthy like us." They all laughed. Two- Feathers smirked at them until they had settled back down.

"So," he began, "you're okay with quicksand ponds then?" Griggs and Hedger shared a cautious look between each other. "How about hidden sinkholes? Not to mention the fire breathing down on us."

"Shut up!" Bowers snapped again.

"I don't know about this," said Kenner. "I say send him back. It's just one guy we're after."

Bowers nodded, thinking it over. Kenner stared intently at him, awaiting his decision.

Two-Feathers moved in close to them. They scowled at him.

"He may be just one guy," said Two-Feathers, "but if it's who I think it is...he knows this area better than anybody and knows how to use it to his advantage."

Bowers spared a quick glance around. Two-Feathers obviously had everyone's attention. He bit at his bottom lip in anger upon seeing Griggs and Hedger were visibly scared, riveted to the chatter of the god damned Indian. He spat and turned his attention back to Two-Feathers.

"Better than you?" he asked.

"Yeah."

Bowers' face was pinched as if he were in the throws of a bad migraine. Then he gave a lilting high pitched laugh and clapped a hand to Two-Feathers back.

"Okay," he said, looked around at the others. "You guys stick to high ground." He glared at Two-Feathers. "You can come with us."

Bowers shoved Two-Feathers toward the edge. He stumbled and cried out as he pitched off the cliff. He grabbed franticly for the vine and seized hold. Two-Feathers shot them an angry glance and began to go down. Bowers grabbed onto it and followed.

Griggs and Hedger started off on foot the other way, passing behind the boulder, and along the high trail.

Two-Feathers looked up and saw them go by. He saw that Kenner had grabbed the vine to come down. The two other men were just too heavy. He could see the limb the vines clung to bowing under the weight. He hurried his pace to get down the vine fast as he could.

An audible CRACK split the calm air. Two-Feathers dropped to the ground. Bowers frowned at him and looked up. Kenner spotted the split in the limb getting larger. Kenner looked down at him, panic stricken eyes bugged out wide.

"Hurry!" he cried. "It's gonna fall!"

The limb gave way a little more. Bowers and Kenner franticly tried to shag the rest of the way down. The limb snapped like a rifle shot and hurtled down.

Bowers and Kenner crashed to the earth on their backs and looked up to see it looming large as it rocketed down. They barely rolled clear. The limb impacted the ground and splintered into flying pieces of debris.

"Son of a bitch!" Kenner yelled, as he dragged himself to his feet. Bowers clambered up and dusted himself off. Two-Feathers held his hands to his stomach and laughed at them hard and loud.

Rain stopped in his tracks. Not far behind him, the echo of the breaking limb and the ensuing crash reached his ears on the wind. He frowned, thought in his head how long he had before they found him here.

He looked ahead at his destination, a sealed doorway, used as an electrician's entrance to the caverns back when only part of the wiring for the roof's lights had been run.

Now the door was rusted and nearly grown over with ivy and brush.

Between Rain and his entrance lay a field of quicksand that marked the edges of the floodplain. The entire hidden lake of it was protruded by cypress stumps, like the multitude spikes of some great armored beast.

He again looked around, up at the skies, and saw the wind blowing the leaves had turned swift and was driving the fire ever more toward the park. The smell of smoke was beginning to be more that a wisp. You could plainly smell it all around.

Rain heard their fall and their laughter and knew he had to get across and get inside, but the quicksand pond was large. He climbed onto a stump of a tree and placed one foot on top of one of the cypress points.

He stood up and balanced with his arms and placed his foot on the next closest cypress. His body shook with the effort of keeping balance. The longer he stayed perched here in the open the greater chance of becoming the only duck in the shooting gallery.

He roved his eyes over the myriad of stumps around and in front and made his move. He navigated the pond quicker and quicker now, with the balance of a big predatory cat, and began to traverse the gap.

Cates was trying to steady himself and hold the flashlight on his target. The nylon cables and pulleys squeaked and squealed with his and Dixon's weight on the line and the pieces of digging equipment tied on as well.

His beam danced and jiggered all over the walls. At last he turned himself and was able to get a better hold on the line. He trained the beam on the floor of the cavern.

"Holy shit," he breathed. "Holy-fucking-shit!"

"What?"

It was Porter. He had stuck his head out over the jagged lip of the hole to see what was causing the excitement. He was going to question them further when his eyes fell on what Cates was looking at. His mouth hung agape.

The banks of the underground river were embedded with golden coins and they were all only partially visible as they had crusted over by sand and mineral deposits. They were everywhere. Probably scattered from their hiding place in the riverbed by floods.

And in the riverbed was a shimmering, sparkling layer of gold as if sunshine were coming from below the rapids, where the rest of the gold lay buried.

"Are you seeing this?" asked Dixon. He laughed

"Yeah," said Porter. "I see."

"It's fucking beautiful!" exclaimed Cates.

"Yes," Porter said, "Truly a thing of beauty...and untold wealth."

Dixon struggled to hold on down below and looked up at Porter. "Are we gonna have enough packs for all of this?" he asked.

Porter shook his head. "Just get as much as you can and fuck all if any is left. We can't come back."

"Looks like our Indian friend was right!" exclaimed Cates.

"So he was," said Porter. "Now get down there and start gathering it up." Porter's head disappeared from the opening. Cates grinned and stared down at Dixon.

He nodded and they quickly worked their way down the ropes.

Kenner and Bowers followed Two-Feathers quickly down the trail, rounded a giant boulder and dropped farther down along the dry river bank. The ground was steadier and more sure footed.

They edged past the face of a sheer rock cliff. Bowers looked up at the trail above. He hoped that Griggs and Hedger could keep up. They kept moving and wound their way past palmetto trees and into a clearing.

Kenner was checking the trail above them once more when he ran into Bower's back. He stepped back and stared at Two-Feathers and Bowers.

"What is it?" he asked. "Why are we stopping?"

"I know where he's headed," said Two-Feathers. He pointed to the overgrowth encrusted door across the cypress field in front of them.

"So what's the problem?" asked Bowers.

"I don't see any tracks."

"Could he have gotten past us?" asked Kenner. "Or climbed up?"

Two-Feathers studied the riverbed. He searched for any sign of foot prints or anything to suggest that Rain had crossed. He shook his head. "Not without us hearing or seeing."

Bowers stared across at the doorway. He tapped Kenner on the arm and started cautiously out into the open. He dropped down off the trail into the riverbed.

"Be careful," cautioned Two-Feathers. Bowers turned and gave him a disgusted sneer.

"Oh, get fucked Wahoo," he said. "I'm getting tired of all the spook stories."

Bowers turned his and back and continued on. When Kenner saw that Bowers had gotten a safe distance out, he moved forward and followed suit. He separated from Bowers by several feet, the both of them shouldering past the poking cypress stumps.

On one of these stumps, on the other side of a broad tree trunk stood Rain, feet apart and balanced, watching as they inched closer. Rain sneered malevolently, intense concentration etched on his face.

"Come on in," he whispered in a dangerous tone. "Closer. Closer."

He knew it was a matter of time. He just had to wait a few more seconds. He thought this must be what it was like for the spider as he waited for the fly.

They came a little farther in, crunching twigs and limbs and dead leaves. Suddenly, Bowers hit a deep slick of quicksand sunk to his waist. He screamed and flailed, and sunk deeper to his chest in an instant.

Kenner whirled around and saw him go down. "No!" he cried. "Hang on man!" Kenner scrambled over a fallen log and nearly plunged himself into the muck as well.

He grabbed hold of Bower's hand and forearm, dropping his weapon on the ground to do so. Rain watched them as they struggled. He pulled a big thick cypress limb up along his side and hoisted it onto his shoulder.

Rain emerged from his cover. He lept onto another trunk, bounding from one stump to the next, and brought up the limb like a hockey player getting ready to strike the puck soaring into the goal.

Bowers looked up, did a double take, and Rain descended on them like a bird of prey. He slammed the club into the side of Kenner's head, crushing it in a spray of blood and bone fragments.

"Oh my god!" yelled Bowers.

Bowers stared, horror struck at the attack, as Kenner's prone body fell forward next to him and began to sink as well. He realized then that he was still armed.

Bowers still clutched his gun. He turned and brought up his arm to fire. Rain side stepped, balanced on another stump and swung the limb across his body, and the blow snapped Bowers gun arm in two.

Bowers cried out in a scream of agony, his broken arm flailing limply. Rain twirled the limb and pushed the bottom of it into Bowers' chest. He glowered down at him, unmoved by his shrieks of protest, as he forced him down.

"No!" screamed Bowers. "No, don't!"

He gargled and sputtered, spitting out the mud, then got forced all the way under by the pole.

The quicksand bubbled three more times and was still. Rain stared down at the pit as he tossed the limb aside.

Rain caught movement to his left and turned quickly. He almost fell. He caught himself and stood straight. He took a long hard look at Two-Feathers as he stood on the bank of the riverbed.

Rain was shocked. He couldn't believe his eyes. He hadn't seen this man since he was a small boy but he knew the son of one of his oldest friends when he saw him.

He used to go bow fishing with Two-Feathers' father when he first became a forest ranger. The two of them must have covered every inch of these woods and in time he taught Rain to know them like the back of his own hand.

"Johnny?" he asked. "Johnny Two-Feathers?" Two-Feathers nodded. Rain relaxed his stance.

"What are you doing here?"

"Their leader," he began, "hired me to show them where the gold is." He could barely meet Rain's gaze. His eyes faltered and he kept them looking at the ground. "My family's gold. My people's gold."

Rain shook his head at the betrayal. He wanted to go to him, but he had to get to the others.

He looked back over his shoulder at the waiting door and then back to Two-Feathers. He knew what was going on with his family. His father's illness and death. Rain was at the funeral.

"What would your father think?" asked Rain.

"I know," said Johnny. "I've sold out my ancestors. I've dishonored them. But we can't pay all dad's medical bills."

Rain's shoulders slumped. He could hear that Two-Feathers was clearly ashamed and could see tears had started to fall. "I'm sorry," said Rain.

Two-Feathers glanced up at him and gave a half smile. He forced himself to meet Rain's eyes.

"When they came to us looking for a guide," he said. "I told them I would do whatever they wanted."

They heard a loud rustling noise and voices. Rain glanced around. He was exposed. Two-Feathers turned half around to check behind him. Griggs and Hedger tore themselves free of the brush at the end of the upper trail and Hedger spotted them. He tapped Griggs on the arm. Two-Feathers whirled back around to Rain.

"Get out of here!" he yelled.

Hedger opened fire. His rounds hit the base of the stump Rain was on and sent him flying. Rain planted one foot on an adjacent stump and managed to stumble from one stump to the next as Hedger and Griggs slid down the hill with guns blazing.

The bullets tore up the ground and split and splintered stumps, narrowly missing Rain's heels as he frantically plunged ahead. A stray bullet hit his radio and busted it into little chunks and shards of plastic and circuitry.

Rain jerked his arm away just in time but kept his focus on his footing. Rain's heart thundered and he kept expecting to plunge headlong into the quicksand mire. He kept his eyes forcused on where to put his feet as debris flew around him.

Two-Feathers tried to grab Kenner's discarded weapon. He fired wildly with it, but it was just the distraction Rain needed, because now the gunmen were focused on him instead.

Hedger cut Two-Feathers down with a quick burst of rounds. Two-Feathers fell back into the pit and began to sink. Griggs was the first to reach the bottom. He got to his feet firing and his bullets tore a jagged chunk out of the large cypress trunk as Rain disappeared behind it.

Rain planted his left foot firmly on the final stump he had and launched himself into the air. He drove his legs in the air trying to power to the other riverbank.

He landed hard, one of his knees planting itself in the muck and he crawled the rest of the way up. He rushed for the abandoned door at a full charge and slammed his shoulder against the metal.

The framing gave way with a crunching sound, like crushing an aluminum soda can in your hand, and the door folded inward enough for him to wedge through.

Griggs and Hedger side stepped along the bank trying to get a clear view and opened fire on the door. Rain barely tucked his head inside when the rounds punched in, perforating the side where the hinges were. Amazingly, they held.

Griggs started to give chase. He was trying to step down off the bank. Hedger grabbed hold of his coat and reined him back in.

"No!" he shouted.

"Why not?"

"It's all quicksand," said Hedger. "Everywhere. We can't get through now."

Griggs stared across the littered path to the doorway. He licked his mouth like a wild dog that tasted blood for the first time and liked it and knew it just wanted some more.

"There's got to be a way," said Griggs. He stared at the door again. "Where does it go?"

"We'll have to find out," said Hedger. "Then we'll get him. Come on."

Rain watched from back inside the cavern, peering out through his wedge of daylight where he tore through. Hedger was already making to climb back up to the trail above. Griggs reluctantly went to join him. The man spared furtive glances his way even as they started to climb the wall.

Rain couldn't help but smile sardonically as he watched them, and rubbed at his sore shoulder. It was the thrill of the hunt. Rain knew it well. He knew that Griggs was tweaking on it. The adrenaline spike.

Rain was tweaking on it too. He was on a collision course now that he had gotten inside. He would let the spike fuel and control his body as he focused his mind on his task at hand. Find Ellie. Find the people. And Porter. He turned away from the door, and the ray of light and prepare to withstand the cold and the damp... in the darkness.

CHAPTER 8

CHOOSING
THE RIGHT PATH

Rain struggled to the top of a rock formation that the old engineers had dubbed, The Squatty Toad. It was a bulging wide spread rock with two small boulders attached near its back side with an elongated and rounded face. It looked like a big brown toad on its belly.

He found before him, three worm holes through the cavern walls. He had no idea where to start. Only a rusted junction box stood on a mostly rotted railroad cross tie to mark the old site of the first cavern electricity.

Due to the area is subjectivty to flooding during the rainy spring season, all other signs had been washed away that might indicate where the engineers went from here.

He shrugged his shoulders and crawled into the first of the holes.

He crawled on hands and knees and came around a jagged corner. The hole began to get smaller. He touched along the sides and could feel the hole closing in around him as the path got decidedly narrower the farther he went.

With a grunt, he managed to back up a few feet and get his body curled to where he could get his feet behind him and crawl back out. Rain emerged from the hole and wiped his slick and sandy hands down the front of his pant legs.

"Let's see what's behind door number two, Bob."

Rain ducked down and wedged himself into the second worm hole. He was going to have a tight squeeze with this one and could only move sideways with his feet pigeon-toed for a distance.

He rounded a curve in the cave walls, stepped over a pile of small rocks, and could see a crawl space up ahead. He worked his way toward it, the small flashlight jitter-ed in his mouth and flickered its faint beam helter-skelter over the walls.

He twisted free of the claustrophobic hole and got down on hands and knees to crawl forward. He took the light from between his teeth and gripped it in his right hand.

He crawled up over a lip in the rock floor and onto a flat spot. He put his hand out to shine the light ahead. Directly in front of his face, a snake rose up and flared it's hooded head, and hissed menacingly at him.

"Ah-ahhh," cried Rain and slid himself backward, nearly falling back down. The snake swayed and lurched in the beam of the light. He should have known it was only a Puff Adder. Even with his years of experience he should have known cobras don't even live in this country, let alone this area of it. But given his present circumstances, who could blame him for freaking out a little?

He took a deep breath and blew it out slowly. The snake seemed to settle down...It went back to crawling on it's belly. Rain shone the beam upward to the top of the crawl space and saw that it had long ago been sealed by a cave-in.

He turned half around and put the beam back on the narrow crack he had just made it through. He sighed and let his head drop tiredly down against his forearm. He lay there just a moment, then with a groan, pushed himself back on his feet.

Porter was checking on things at the dig. He watched as two more men, Sully and Owens pulled another pack up from the hole. This made four so far, each weighed down to the bursting point with salvaged gold.

He was admiring the shine and the glimmer it gave off, even in the dim light of the caverns, and was reaching down to pick up a handful for a closer look. Then his walkie crackled to life. Porter grabbed it.

"Tell me good news," he said.

"We have none, sir," It was Hedger's voice. "Kenner and Bowers are dead." Porter clenched his eyes shut, hit by a sudden migraine. "The Indian too."

"No big waste," Porter managed to reply. "We're moving along nicely here. Keep tracking him and keep me posted."

There was a pregnant pause on the other end. Porter was beginning to think they didn't hear him. He was getting ready to speak again when Hedger came back on.

"That's why we called, sir," he began. "He's inside."

"What?" asked Porter, incredulously. "How?"

"An old entrance, along the floodplain. We can't get to it. You got any ideas?"

Porter rubbed furiously at his temples with his thumb and fingertips. He didn't answer them. How could this have turned into such a disaster? It was supposed to be simple. He should have known that nothing ever really was. He jumped at the static noise of the radio as Hedger called back.

"Porter?" Hedger prompted. "Any ideas? Over."

"One," replied Porter coldly. Then he shut off his radio before they could irritate him further.

An endless stream of panicked thoughts raced through Ellie's mind. Porter had come in to talk to her again. She could tell by the way his body talked that he was fit to be tied. Was Rain all right? Was he dead? Did he get inside?

Each thought cannibalized the others before she could feel the emotion they carried. Here he was, the son of a bitch, with another icy stare that insisted you look him in the eyes no matter how much it knotted up your insides.

"The forest ranger," he began, "it seems, has found his way in."

That answered one of her questions for her. Two in fact. He was inside the caverns somehow and that meant he was very much alive. She still couldn't believe he came back. She doubted very much that it was for her. The fire must have taken a turn sooner than anyone expected.

"Do you know anything about the floodplain entrance?" he inquired. Barely contained menace seasoned his voice to a biting quality. "Where will he go from there?"

He cocked his head sideways and moved it closer to her face. God, how he looked so snake like it made her skin positively crawl. She forced herself to maintain eye contact. If she didn't, she feared he would think her a liar. She truly believed what she said next, because it was the truth.

"I don't know," she stated.

Porter bared his teeth and seized a handful of her hair. He pulled hard and she cried out. He began to pull so hard, Ellie thought he was going to tear a hunk of hair right out of her head along with the skin attached to it. She screamed. The little girl, Sue, ran to her aid.

"Leave her alone!" she shrieked.

"Shut up, little bitch!" he yelled back. Her brother Robbie grabbed her around the middle and tried to drag her away. He got her to a safe distance. He and Porter glared at each other. Porter turned back to Ellie. He let her hair go but stayed right in her face.

"Tell me what you know!" he exclaimed. "No more lies!"

"I swear I have no clue!" she cried. "That was sealed off years ago when the first electricity was run here."

She tried her best to regain her poise. It wasn't easy. She feared for the children's safety most now. As insane as this man was, she had no misconception that he could kill children and easily as anybody else, if it came down to it.

"There may be worm holes through the rock," she said. "I'm not sure where they go."

She shook her head to further emphasize her doubt. Porter shoved her away. He turned to Sully and Owens whom he had brought with him for the interrogation. They were eyeing her with disdain.

"I hate to have bugs behind my walls...all that scratching around," he told Sully. "See if you can follow any cables to that entrance and get rid of that bastard Ranger."

They had started to back away a little and exchange a questioning look, not certain if he was finished with them. Porter gave them a look as if he wondered what they were doing still standing there. He advanced on them rapidly.

"Now!" he barked. "God damn today!"

The two men scurried off. Flashlight beams danced across the ceiling as they ran, They tried to follow the cables that snaked along the ceilings of the room and out the entry way.

Tatum had driven out of the burn zone and parked at the lookout point where the highest forestry tower in the state stood like steel cyclops on its four legs with its southward facing window that gleamed in the sunlight.

He had climbed up to watch the progress of the conflagration of flame as it marched unstoppable, ever upward. The county crews were losing the battle. Losing? Hell, they never had a fucking chance once that tanker blew up. Then it was all over but the crying.

He tried to help. He tried to do what Rain had urged him to do. To do anything he could. Now he wasn't so sure of his decision. He wasn't so sure he should have set that backfire.

He looked toward the direction of the park. The wind had kicked up a notch as it often did this time of day and the ever blacken smoke of where his fire and the monster blaze were joined had begun to carry on the wind. The wind also fed and drove the fire and soon it would be on them and all around. There would be no way out.

He had to do something. Sitting up here on his ass was doing nothing to help. He groaned as he got up from the wooden chair. He stole another glance out the window and reached down to open the floor hatch. The ground was along way down and he made his way there.

Tatum's fire whipped through the dried trees, toward the larger blaze. A wind gust merged the two and they coiled in their infernal embrace like incendiary lovers.

An eruption of fire and sparks blasted out with the wind behind it and decimated a football field sized stand of pines. The pure lighter that comes in pine wood only added un-needed fuel.

The larger inferno began to churn thick black smoke as the two fires were officially made one, and began its inevitable turn directly for the park.

A coyote flushed from its hole ran toward a family of fleeing rabbits and hurtled them. Hunger could wait. Everything was burning down, all their homes, and he was getting away. Five deer bounded away from a cluster of brush seconds before it ignited and they ran as fast as their strong legs could carry them.

Rain searched with the toe of his boot incessantly and finally got footing on a small rock outcropping. He crawled along on his belly. His small flashlight cast its beam all around the tube he was wedged into.

The beam caught in its glare an albino spider, typical for caves like these, that hung from a single strand of web silk. Rain flicked it aside with his light and continued on. He was drenched in sweat from the effort of having to crawl and climb most of the way on his stomach.

He was perched on the brink of breakdown. His muscles trembled from exhaustion. His mind itself seemed to ache with effort. He rounded a bend in the crawl space and his light shone on a widening at the next turn. He allowed himself a hopeful raise of the eyebrows. It looked as if it might be big enough to stand.

Rain pushed harder. He felt like a baby trying to come out the wrong way. It was beyond taxing to go at this pace. His eyes fluttered as he faught the nausea of both claustrophobia and the strain this was taking on him.

Rain rounded the final bend and began to struggle to get to hands and knees. Eventually he was able to stand although bent nearly half way over. He shined the light around and off to his left was one of the original breaker boxes.

This one was less rusted and seemed to be in good working order. There, on the roof, were cables. He had found the start of the old wiring system. Now he was in business. All he had to do was follow it and it would take him where he needed to be.

He stood there a moment and thought of Ellie. She had held onto his hand in a lingering way, and although she was fighting back the tears that threatened to fall, he could still see behind them, that there was still a hope, that he would rethink the situation. Still the hope of it not being over. Not truly.

Rain's breath hitched in his lungs and his eyes watered over a moment. He coughed and forced himself to breath normally again. Forget that for now. There will be time for all that later. He knew he had to stay in the frame of mind of battle.

So he allowed himself one more brief thought of Ellie. Then he steadied himself with a deep, long breath. The shark-eyed intensity was back in his eyes and his features once more taught and steely. He headed off in the direction of the wiring.

CHAPTER 9

GAMES OF CAT AND MOUSE

Sully and Owens had followed the cables on the ceilings from one end of the caverns to the other. So far, they had found nothing. They had lamented ever tying in with Porter on this job. The bastard was incorrigible enough as it was and being stuck with him in a dark bunch of caves made it even worse.

They followed the winding cable through the Cathedral Room, past the large church spire columns and the pipe organ formations and down the path to low passage way.

They had to duck down as low as they could in order to pass through. Sully nearly fell flat on his face when he ducked suddenly to avoid a rock protrusion on the roof of the passage. They stumbled out the other side in an opening.

They were standing in an anti-chamber now. Up above them was the Reflecting Pool room where a pool of crystal clear water from the river below them fills a tub like basin.

Sully was busy cleaning himself off after dragging a leg in that small space they came out of. Owens was the first to discover what they hoped would be useful.

"Hey," he said and tapped Sully. Sully frowned at him and that's when Owens put his flashlight beam on the roof. "Wiring runs in two directions."

"Which way?" asked Sully.

"No way to tell unless we split up," replied Owens. "Looks like the asshole's hunch was right."

Sully nodded. He saw the wiring lead quite aways to his right into another cavern room. "I'll go right," he said, then gestured to Owens by tipping his chin up. "You check up there."

"You got it," said Owens. He flicked his wrist and cast his light beam across the ceiling and the cables that way. He turned away from Sully and started up a pathway that led to the Reflecting Pool room.

"Find anything or anybody strange," began Sully, "you give a yell. All right?" Owens glanced down and gave a single nod. Sully darted off to the right and out of sight. His flashlight beam quickly dwindled away.

Ellie had regained as much composure as she dared to show, given the guards still passed by the ends of this room. Not to mention Porter could rear his ugly head at any given moment.

She knew that Rain was inside. That there was a chance of getting out of this now, had begun to grow in her mind, and in her heart as well. She needed to get to him somehow. Maybe she could help him.

She fought with herself, debated back and forth about slipping away. She could find a worm hole in the walls and make off unnoticed. God knows, she and Rain had explored enough of them on their own. They also did quite a bit more exploring than that down here. She blushed at her memories.

She watched the guard closest to them all pass by the entrance. He never so much as glanced their way. They were getting complacent. That would be a big help to her if they could stay that way for a while longer.

Ellie checked behind her at a large crack in the wall. She knew that one led out of here. She could be three rooms away form here in a couple of minutes and no one would be the wiser.

Then she thought about everybody here. What would be their fate if Porter came back in another manic rage and found her gone. Would he kill them? Probably so. They all looked so tired and hopeless. A lot of them were in the midst of restless sleep while others simply held each other.

Sue and Robbie were watching her closely. Robbie's brow was furrowed in a deep frowning fashion. He evidently figured out what she was turning over in her head. Sue was giving her that "What?" look.

She knew then that if she did try to leave without talking to them about it, that they would follow after her, whether she wanted them to or not. She checked the guards again and then beckoned Sue to her.

Sue also checked the entry ways and edged over to her. Robbie crouched closer to them, just enough to hear. "Sue," she began, "there's somebody trying to help us."

"Really?" she squealed. Robbie winced. Ellie held a finger to her lips to shush her. Ellie nodded.

"Yes," she said. "I have to try and find him."

Sue gave a frightened look at the thought of being left behind. She clutched her hands on Ellie's and looked into her eyes, pleading.

"It won't be long," said Ellie. "Just a few minutes. But I need your help. Will you do something for me?"

Sue pursed her lips. She was thinking it through. Ellie looked at Robbie. Sue met Robbie's gaze and the boy nodded. He glanced at Ellie. "We'll help." he said. Sue nodded her head.

"Sure." she said. "Whatever you need."

"Come with me."

Rain staggered out form a jagged gash filled gully and stood clutching his side and panted as he struggled to fight the burning of his lungs and cool them with gulps of air.

Little by little, the claustrophobic frightened sensation developed from crawling, climbing and squeezing his way through worm holes began to abate. The stitch in his side was also going away. He rubbed furiously at it and groaned as he tried to massage away the last of discomfort.

He bent at the waist and placed his palms on his knees. He rolled his back up and down to stretch it out and the the bones gave some resounding cracks. He began to feel brand new again, relaxed even, until he heard a noise.

The sound of scuffling footsteps came his way and the faint shimmer of flashlight beams on the ceiling and walls of the cavern. It came from below him. Someone was coming up the ramp way to the room he was standing in.

"Shit!" Rain softly whispered, practically hissed, as he looked around frantic to find cover. He put his back against the large sand stone basin that held the reflecting pool. As he turned his head right to search for cover, his features returned from the pool as if he were standing before a mirror.

He could go back into the crevices and hide there. It would probably be safer if he did. Then he could skulk about some more and find out what was really going on. But he didn't want to hide or skulk. He wanted to hunt and wanted to kill. He snarled as he watched light emerge from the tunnel followed by Owens, then he chose his cover and waited to pounce.

Owens shone his beam all around and passed it overhead. Hundreds of thousands of small stalactites dangled from the roof in the foyer, a little display they called New York City upside down on the tour. It looked like the skyline. Owens spotlighted the tag and read this.

He turned his beam back to the ceiling and began to follow the wiring up the walkway toward the stone basin. He moved past it, glanced from floor to ceiling, and checked his footing. It was slick here from all the dripping water from the roof and he nearly went down.

He glanced over at the pool. He did a double take. There he was! He caught a glimpse of Rain at the bottom of the pool. Talk about shooting fish in a barrel.

Owens unslung his machine gun and fired a burst of rounds into the water.

"Got'cha, motherfucker!" he yelled. "I got'cha!"

He stopped firing and swung the barrel of his gun left and right, searching. He had disappeared!

"What the..." was all he could manage. Rain dropped from the ceiling above him, wrapped Owens in his arms, and dragged him down into the water. Owens kicked and trashed wildly, but Rain grip was far too strong, and suddenly the splashing stopped.

Rain emerged from the pool and sucked in a deep breath. He slung an arm over the side of the basin and used it to haul himself out. He dropped down on one knee and breathed heavily.

That was one down. How many more to go? Rain knew one thing, he didn't care what the answer to that was. All that mattered now was finding Ellie. He had to move. He had a feeling Owens was no lone scout. He was armed for bear.

Sully stopped in his tracks upon hearing the burst of rounds go off in the distance. The echo was still coming to him seconds later. He listened and heard nothing else. He grabbed his radio from his belt.

"We got him!" he exclaimed. "Owens got the son of a bitch!"

Porter pulled his own radio from his pocket and listened to the news. He smiled inspite of his best efforts not to. He forced himself to remember that nothing could be left to chance in a situation like this. The old sternness returned.

"You better be sure," he cautioned. "Go round up Owens and you two get back here. We got what we came for and we need to shag ass."

Cates and Dixon climbed out of the hole. Porter nodded to them. They had returned with two more of the packs loaded with gold coins.

"Yes, sir," was Sully's reply.

Porter tucked away the radio. One of the coins fell out from one of the sacks and landed near Porter's feet.

It was facing heads up. He nodded. Perhaps luck was going to be on his side after all.

Porter bent and picked this one up. He ran his fingertips over the mineral crusted part and the shiny gold part of the coin with the gentle caress of a lover. He put it gingerly in his pocket and patted it.

He turned away from the hole as Royce began to emerge, dragging equipment behind him. He needed to deliver a message to that bitch tour guide. "This should take the fucking wind out of her sails," he thought.

Porter walked down the corridor and turned left, crossed the anti-chamber and came to the entrance of the hostage room. He poked his head in around the wing. There she was, sitting on a rock with her back to him. Fine. He could do without seeing her face anyway.

"I just thought you should know," he chided, "helps not coming."

He watched with the utmost satisfaction as she slumped her shoulders. She was crushed. For once, she had nothing to fire back at him. Oh, how he loved having the upper hand. There was simply nothing else like it in the world.

He chuckled and turned away form the entry. Dillon, this end's guard, marched by right behind him. Whispered out bursts of anger and whined pleading broke among the hostages. Sue listened, she sat there on the rock, while tears streamed down her face and soaked Ellie's tour shirt, and listened to their worry and woe.

Rain made his way down the path that Owens had used to come up to this room. He kept himself flattened along the wall as much as possible and tried to move quietly on the balls of his feet. No sound.

He thought he heard something. He stopped and listened for a moment, his head tilted left and right like a predatory bird, as he tried to discern the direction of the movement.

He dashed out into the open. He froze in place upon seeing Ellie standing in the path ahead. She never saw him. Thoughts of earlier today when they were prepared to go there separate ways came to him. They were so trivial. Now that he glimpsed her again he only wanted to keep seeing her forever.

He started stealthily toward her, nearly dared to call out to her, when she was caught in the beam of a light and heavy footsteps thudded toward her.

Ellie turned to the light and tried to shield her eyes with a forearm. Sully had caught her sneaking.

"What are you doing here?" he demanded.

Rain saw another path to his right. He wedged in behind a row of columns that flanked Sully.

He began to slowly work his way around. He crept by them, not taking his eyes off them. Not taking his eyes off Ellie.

"I said what are you doing!" snapped Sully.

Ellie spotted Rain behind the columns. He gave her a stern glare to urge her to keep his secret. He was nearly behind Sully now.

"I was trying to escape," she said.

Sully had to laugh. Her flippant, yet honest reply, took him off his game for a second. Just for a second. "There won't be any escaping," he stated. Sully unslung his machine gun and cocked the safety back. Suddenly two large meaty hands seized him by the forehead and chin.

Rain twisted Sully head. Ellie looked away as the man's neck snapped with a sickening crunch, like dry kindling wood. Sully fell to the floor in a crumpled pile.

"Not for you anyway," said Rain.

Ellie ran to him and threw herself into his arms. He embraced her strongly and held onto her, and tears streamed from their eyes. Rain sat her back on her feet.

They stood there and looked at each other for the longest time. They had goofy grins that appeared on their faces and then disappeared just as quickly. They stared at each other as if they had not seen each other in years, not mere hours.

"I'm glad you're here," she sobbed. "I hoped it was you."

"It's okay," he said. "I'm sorry for earlier."

Ellie shook her head. She was bewildered. She wiped the tears from her face with the back of her hands and her features completely softened.

"You never apologize," she said. "Never, in all the time I've known you."

Rain shrugged his shoulders. He managed to give her his best smile under the circumstances.

"I figured now was as good a time as any."

He tried not to laugh and cry at the same time. Tears filled his eyes but he bit at both his lips to stop the broad grin that threatened to break out. She laughed. It was a high, nervous tittle of laughter, but he would take it. They might be on their way to all right, if they could get out of this.

"Where are the others?" he asked.

"Christmas Room," she answered.

"How many more men?"

"Four or five," she said. She tried to think. "There's Porter too, so maybe as many as six."

Rain couldn't help watching her. She paced back and forth in front of him and he admired every inch of her. She always was his perfect woman since the first time he saw her. He frowned.

He couldn't believe he was headed for California not long ago.

"There's two more outside." he said. "I lost them earlier."

Sully's radio crackled to life. They stared down at it as Porter's voice came to them from it.

"Sully! Owens!" he called. "Where the hell are you?"

Ellie looked down at the radio with such disdain, as if touching it would put her back in the clutches of that horrid man. Rain sneered. He bent and plucked the radio from the dead man's belt. "Get back to the hole!"

"They're not gonna make it." Rain gravely entered. Porter was not thrown off for an instant, even as menacing as Rain was, because he came right back at them.

"Oh, really?" he asked. "You must be the forest ranger that's causing all the trouble." Rain grew angrier the longer Porter went on. His entire hand had turned white from grasping the radio so hard.

"Are you there?"

"Yeah," said Rain. "I am."

"How fucking lovely..."

Rain dropped the radio on the ground and stomped on it. That closed Porter's mouth figuratively. Now he only had to do it literally. Rain looked forward to the time.

Porter jerked the radio away from his ear. Static practically screamed at him. He shut it off and lowered it down to his side. He pursed his lips together. So now it has begun. The ranger was going to insist of a course of action Porter could not hold with.

He could see that he had to be dealt with. On the other hand, if all went according to plan, the fire should be closing on them and they had little time left for a clean getaway.

Price, one of his floating guard detail watched him with a hawk like intensity. Porter paid him little mind. What could he do to fix this broken axle and get rolling again? Price, as if reading his mind, spoke up.

"What do we do now?" he asked.

"We have little time. We have to grab the gold and move."

Porter stalked the room like a big cat in his cage growing more and more agitated by the second. He shot Price a shark-eyed glare that made the man flinch.

"We hunt him down," said Porter. "There's nowhere to go."

Porter turned on his heels and tramped across the fragile cavern floor to the hostage area.

"And just to make sure he's a good boy..."

Porter entered the hostage chamber. He walked quickly over to Ellie and jerked her up by the collar. The park guide shirt slide off and was all he clutched in his clinched fist.

Sue was left standing there where he thought he would find Ellie. Porter's color drained from his cheeks and all his features were taut as a tightrope. Porter was positively livid.

Porter made a move toward her and Sue whimpered. She dropped to the ground and crawled away. Porter glanced from her to the shirt and to Price. Dillon the other guard on duty had joined them. He shook the shirt at them.

"How did she..." Dillon looked dumbfounded by the shirt in Porter's white knuckle grip. He just shook his head slowly back and forth.

"I don't know," he said. "I've been here the whole time. So was Price." Porter looked up at Price and met his gaze. Price nodded.

"Fuck!" screamed Porter. "Fuck! Everybody spread out and find them."

He trudged over to Dillon. The man started to back away and thought it better to stay and bear the brunt of Porter's anger rather than have to deal with him later. Porter got right in his face.

"Try," he rasped, "keeping your eyes open this time. Would you?"

Porter shoved him back and stalked away to join his men at the hole. Royce stood by him while Price led the others away, their flashlights shining, all guns drawn and ready.

Rain and Ellie had made their way into the best worm holes of the caverns. They didn't have to crawl here. There was at least standing room even if there were tight squeezes in some places.

They moved sideways one behind the other, through the narrow crevice behind the wall. They made their way as quickly as they could, felt along the walls with their hands and felt for obstacles on the floor with their feet.

They didn't have to use the flashlight back here. There were holes in the wall and any light they shed might be spotted by those inside the cavern. They could hear Porter and his men as the scuttled and scurried all over the caves. The strange tonality of hearing it on their side of the wall made it sound like the meanderings of large bugs.

Rain's foot kicked a rock and sent it bouncing off the wall of the cavern with a hollow thud. It sounded as if he dropped a small boulder on the floor. Flashlight beams bathed the interior ceiling in yellow light. Rain clenched his teeth in anger.

"Over here," shouted Royce. "I heard something!"

Rain held a hand out to steady Ellie. There was a hole barely above their heads. If someone were to get up to it they could see right in. Flashlight beams shone through it. Rain grabbed Ellie and they ducked swiftly and silently down.

The light beams faded and went away. They stood back up again and dared not move. They could still hear the men shuffling toward their location. Rain could see out a sliver of a crack and flinched back when he saw Porter arrive right in front of him.

He clenched his hands tightly against the wall behind him. How he wanted to get his hands on Porter. He wanted it so bad he could nearly taste it. Ellie must have sensed his emotions because she was staring at him and she squeezed his meaty forearm once.

"What was it?" asked Porter. "Could one of these stupid rocks have fallen?" He shined his light all around the top of the ceiling where the stalactites grew.

"Probably," sighed Royce. "I guess it was nothing."

Porter nodded. He flashed his light around the room once more, then waved them all off. He gestured at Cates and Dixon, two of his men from the dig site.

"You two go that way," he said. He pointed to a pathway off to their far right. "Everybody else, get moving."

Rain and Ellie shared a look, then listened, as all the men began to spread at through the caves Rain watched through the crack. His stare must have been intense.

Porter stopped and turned back around. He stared at the crack and this made Rain flinch again. There was no way he could see him. Maybe Porter only felt him. The way you feel it when you know someone is watching you.

Porter started for the crack. He aimed to peer inside. Rain could see him advancing and knew any second the game was over. Ellie tightened her grip on Rain's arm.

Porter touched the wall and prepared to bring his eye to the fissure. That instant, Royce ran back into the room and Porter turned to him.

"We've found Sully," he said. "His neck's been snapped."

"Christ!" hissed Porter.

Porter turned from the wall and ran to join Royce at the tunnel that led out of the room. Royce ran on ahead with Porter on his heels.

Ellie nudged Rain and urged him to move. They wormed their way faster now, but still careful of their movements. They could hear the footfalls of Royce and Porter rapidly moving away, and the faintest sound of garbled exclamations from the other men. Rain thought these must have found the other guy he drowned.

Porter and Royce joined the others. Flashlight beams landed all over the body of Sully and revealed the vicious wrenching the man's neck sustained at Rain's grip.

"He nearly got his damn head ripped off." marveled Royce.

Porter merely nodded. Royce stared at him. Porter turned away to think. What could possibly be driving this man? There were no two ways about it. Porter knew he would have to face the ranger and he would not come out unscathed. He would come out of it for the better though. Of that, he was certain.

Fresh cries of fear and excitement snapped him quickly out of his reverie. The shock of the out cries was like a slap in the face while you were sleeping. He started and then trailed after Royce, Dixon, and Cates as they started up a trail leading to a floor above.

The others were standing at a large rock basin and shined their flashlights inside. Porter shoved the others aside and peered down at the floating body of Owens. His face was a frozen mask of surprise and horror.

"What are we gonna do?" Royce practically demanded.

Porter shook his head. His thoughts wouldn't stop spinning around in there and he needed to gain control. Royce advanced on him yet again and the others looked on with mild curiosity.

"Who knows how many more of our men he's taken out," said Royce. "I'm beginning to wonder if we're all next." He cornered Porter, forcing him to stop his incessant pacing. "This isn't worth my life," he said and turned to the others. "I say we cut and run!"

Porter's eyes flashed silver with anger. He lashed out and clamped his hands on Royce's head.

He pushed his thumbs over the man's eyelids and applied the pressure. The others turned away to avoid seeing.

Royce dropped his light on the ground and his weapon slid off his shoulder and clattered to the cavern floor. He swatted at his own face and Porter's forearms as Porter increased the vice grip on his skull.

Porter's thumbs pressed down harder still. Royce screamed as he felt his eyeballs compressed in their sockets. It felt that they would squirt out from under Porter's thumbs at any second.

"You must see," began Porter, "that it's just one man." He shook Royce violently by his head and applied more pressure. This illicited a high pitched whine from him. "And we have all our friends here with us to lend a hand."

Royce had dropped to his knees now. Porter refused to ease up. Dixon and Cates stared, slack jawed, as their leader taught his lesson in violence.

"You do see that, don't you?" Porter asked. "Do you see?"

"Yes!" screamed Royce. "For Christ's sake, yes! I fuckin' see!"

Porter shoved him away. Royce fell onto his back. He jutted his legs out from underneath him so he could roll onto his side. He cradled his aching eyes in his palms and curled into a fetal position.

Porter looked down at him and managed to smile. He stood tall and breathed deeply as he watched Royce soothe himself. He looked over at Cates and Dixon.

They straightened themselves before him and now Royce was getting to his feet. When he was up and watched Porter through streaming tears, Porter strolled casually up to them. He had gained control over the situation, yet again.

"So," he began, "The hunt continues?"

CHAPTER 10

THE HUNT CONTINUES

Ellie and Rain were now where they could move freely. They skirted a boulder pile where part of the roof had collapsed many years ago. Rain darted ahead, quietly on the balls of his feet, and passed behind another section of wall, slick and blackened by mineral water trickling from overhead.

They came to an area that revealed an opening in the wall. Red light cast a pale crimson glow on the dirt at the entrance to the hostage chamber, The Christmas Room. They made it.

Rain held up a hand and stopped Ellie. He pointed through a hole in the rocks where they caught a glimpse of Dillon as he passed through the room amid the hostages. He swept his light and his gun back and forth as he checked for movement.

Rain ducked down and moved forward, close to the exit of their worm hole. He watched Dillon leave the Christmas Room and watch his shadow fleet across the dim lit walls of the outside corridor.

Rain took the lead again. He and Ellie emerged from their crack in the wall and stepped into the room. Sue and Robbie spotted them first and Sue got to her feet, about to call out, and Ellie put a finger over her lips in a shushing motion.

They nodded. Rain glanced at the kids and moved away from Ellie. Other hostages had gotten a look at him and begun to stir. Ellie waved her arms at them to stay where they were and Sue mimicked her shushing gesture.

Rain shadowed Dillon. He watched the man's shadow as it drifted over the walls and listened to the lazy shuffle of his booted feet as the man led them away from the hostages.

They were entering the dig site. The light was brighter here. Dillon crossed the room and stood at the hole in the floor. He peered over the edge at the rapid river below him. The way the light was shining so brightly there was no way the man would see Rain come.

A rope slipped over Dillon's head and tightened around his throat. The man's face went straight to purple from the strength of Rain's grip. Dillon dropped his weapon and light and clawed at his neck. Rain let go and shoved him over the edge of the hole.

Dillon fell toward the water screaming. The rope of the lowering rig drew taut and hanged him. His feet kicked at the top of the water. His body spasmed as he rapidly ran out of air and did the dance of death.

Rain glared down at him from the edge of the hole. He whirled around as Ellie rushed into the room. He embraced her and they stayed that way an instant longer. They seperated and looked down at the ground. There were four big rucksacks loaded with encrusted gold coins.

"What's the quickest way out?" asked Rain.

"There's a hole in the roof," began Ellie, "in the room to our left. It's where the escavaters dug through years ago. Punch through that and you're outside."

Rain nodded. Ellie bent and picked up a small pick axe and a hammer laying at their feet. Rain couldn't help but admire her. She was so courageous. That's probably one of the things that attracted him to her more than any other, her fearlessness.

"I'll go hold them off," said Rain. He grabbed her soft shoulders in his gnarled strong hands. "Can you get them out?"

"Yeah," she said and nodded. Rain smiled at her and clapped her on the upperarm.

"Okay," he said. "Go!"

Sue and Robbie had come looking for her. She grabbed them by their hands and led them back the way they came. Sue looked back and smiled at him. Rain managed a smile back, but he was worried about them. If he could keep the men distracted they might make it.

Rain kept his intense eyes wide and focused as he glared down the passage way before him. He tried to sharpen that determined thousand yard stare and force, will, his desire for vengeance to spread out and permeate to the rocks. He wanted Porter to feel him coming now.

"Okay everybody," he heard Ellie say, "Let's go. Quietly, please! Follow me! Quickly!"

Ellie led them past Rain. A few people gave him wary looks, some looks of awe. Others were relieved to be moving. Rain knew they hoped for a way out. He did not return their gaze as Ellie led them away. He kept his gaze locked down the dark chamber.

The last of the hostages entered the chamber to the left and disappeared from view. Rain broke away, and sprinted lightly and swiftly, down the dark tunnel and deeper into the cavern.

Ellie stood in the center of the chamber. The hostages were milling around fretfully, crammed together in the small cone shaped room. Sue and Robbie were holding her hands as she peered at the small cylindrical dome at the top.

It was sealed back up after the engineers had tunneled far enough in to make other paths and tunnels. She knew that a few stabs with the pick axe may break the sand stone plug loose. She put her head down and closed her eyes a moment in brief prayer.

"Okay," she said and glanced from Sue to Robbie and back again. "Here we go."

She placed her foot on a small boulder that marked the old debris pile she turned to all the others and gestured with the wave of an arm as she said, "Everybody stand back aways." She pointed with her flashlight to show them the roof. "I'm going to try and break that down."

She made her way carefully up the loose rock pit. She lost footing once and nearly pitched off to the side but she battled on. She reached the top of the slide and began to chip away at the soft rock. She shielded her face with her free arm as pieces began to fall away.

She was getting tired, already. It was hard as hell to swing the pick axe up at this angle and her arm was burning with fire deep in the muscle and her rotater cuff began to twinge.

One more stroke of the pick axe and a hole appeared in the dome. Brighter daylight filtered down on her face outside. She looked down at her haggard group and smiled.

"It's working!" she cried. Sue and Robbie jumped up and down and squealed with joy. Ellie shed a couple of tears and turned back to the hole she made. With now found determination and energy, she swung the pick-axe as hard as she could to widen the hole.

Outside the caverns, Hedger and Griggs searched the forest for sign of where Rain could have went. Hedger coughed, hard and hackish, as he looked all around. The smoke was thick now. The fire must be closing on them fast.

Griggs was wiping his shoes. The smoke was getting to him as well and his nose wouldn't stop running. He scowled and stopped mid wipe as the sharp striking sound of metal on rock came to his ears on the wind.

"Hey!" he barked. Hedger whirled on him and raised his hands as if to say, "What gives?" Griggs pointed to their left.

"Did you hear that?" he asked.

They stopped talking and waited to hear anything more. CHINK. There it was. Then again, as Ellie chipped away at the hole. Griggs made a cutting motion with his hand to show Hedger he wanted him to move that direction.

They split off from each other and separated by a few feet as they advanced into a thicket that ringed a small knoll off to their left. They looked at each other and nodded. Ellie's voice came to them. "Any minute now." she said. Hedger watched a chunk of rock fly up from the top of the knoll.

Rain came to a sudden stop, poised still as a statue in the middle of the passage, and watched as flashlight beams bounced off the slick walls and ceilings of a lower cavern chamber. It lay ahead of him and to the right.

Rain smiled, nearly smirked, as he watched them turn his direction. He simply strode forward. He knew where he was, and more importantly, he knew where they were. He had hoped to find them sooner rather than later. Especially right here.

Rain came to a landing just before the floor fell at an angle into a lower chamber. The position offered him safety and a place to run, but more than that, it put him in full view with the dim ceiling light cast behind him. There was no way they could miss him once they rounded another bend.

Porter and Royce were at the lead of their pack of dogs. Royce shone his light around the floor and it landed on Rain's booted feet. He followed the feet and legs up with the light until Rain was caught in the beam.

It wasn't blinding him. The darkness was so thick in the lower chamber that the flashlight was nearly powerless to cut through the pitch black surroundings. Porter grinned like a Cheshire cat. Rain smiled a little.

He had to, the man was so arrogant it was almost funny to him.

The others fell in with their leader and trained their beams on Rain as well. They clicked safety switches on their weapons and took aim, ready to fire if Rain dared so much as twitch. The smile stayed firmly on Rain's face and Porter's grin faltered only slightly.

"Why the devil are you so happy?" asked Porter. "The way I figure it, the end has came for you."

Rain's smile broadened into a malice filled grin. Royce saw and shot Porter an uneasy look. Porter lazily waved a hand at him in a gesture of placation. It was almost like what you would do for someone who was merely slow and couldn't help it.

"Look up." suggested Rain.

Porter blinked. Of all possible responses he could have imagined or even entertained, being told to look up, was not one of them. Not even close. He gave Rain a questioning stare, then the cheshire cat grin was back in place.

"What?" Porter asked. "Why would I want to do that?" Rain shrugged. Dixon and Cates exchanged bewildered looks.

"For shits and giggles," chimed Rain. He smiled again. "Look up."

Porter scowled at him. He nodded at Royce who was staring at him with the wildest eyes he had ever seen. With a shaking hand, Royce lifted his light beam to the cave ceiling as did Price and Holland. The ceiling was covered with what appeared to be rolling mounds of brown shag carpet.

Then it began to move and twitch. A massive cloud of brown cave bats stirred from slumber as the light awakened them. They emitted a high pitched cry in unison and took flight straight down at them like hairy little kamikaze bombers.

Royce screamed in terror and brought his gun up. He dropped his flashlight and it busted on the rocks around but he managed to open fire. He stumbled away and continued to spend round after round.

The other men began to yell and scream as they flailed at the swarm of wings and sharp teeth their lights had unleashed. Porter threw himself to the ground to avoid stray bullets that strafed the air.

A couple of rounds punched into the rock in front of Rain's feet. Rain stumbled away, and shielded his face from razor sharp flying bits of rock. Price and Holland tried to seek cover and Price got taken down by a round through the neck. Blood spurted from beneath his fingers and he fell hard.

Three of the bats were hit dead center and exploded in smoking bits of blood, guts and fur. Porter rolled on to his side and scooped up Price's gun as it clattered across the floor toward him. He saw Rain disappear from view the second before he opened fire on Royce.

Porter's rounds dug a bloody trench up Royce's front from neck to nuts and took the crazed man off his feet. The bats still swarmed about the cave, exiting a few more every turn around the room, confused even more by what was happening in their den.

Porter made it over to Holland who had a superficial wound in the meat of his upper right arm and the two belly crawled out of the room. To avoid the rest of the angry swarm Dixon and Cates had made it out and helped them to their feet at the back of the chamber.

"Shit!" Porter swore. Now they were forced to go the long way around to even get back to the hostages and the gold. That ranger was going to have to pay for this with buckets of blood. He told himself he would see to that before he was done. Buckets of blood.

Porter slapped at his neck and touched his face, anywhere skin was bare, and checked his palms for blood stain. He had not been bitten or scratched. That was a point to the good. He shoved Dixon and Cates ahead.

"Let's get the gold and get out of here!" he yelled. "Maybe we can take that bastard out in the bargain."

Rain took advantage of the chaos that fell in the wake of Royce's freak out. He saw the smugness drop from the visage of Porter and he thrilled that he had gotten the best of him this time.

He hung around long enough to see that and he was off, racing through dark tunnels and narrow crevices, back to the dig site. The gold was what Porter wanted more than anything. What he had proved he was willing to kill for.

Ellie, with any luck had all the hostages out of the caverns, so they were safe for the mean time, If they were to stay safe, however, Rain knew he had to get the gold out as well and that he had to keep it out of Porter's grasp.

Rain grabbed two of the stuffed rucksacks and pulled them onto his shoulder to hang at the apex of his broad back. He shrugged the next two bags onto his shoulders and felt them sag under the considerable weight. Each one of these had to weigh nearly a hundred pounds.

There had to be much more down there, but what he bore on his sturdy frame right now was worth hundreds of millions of dollars. Given how old it was and the adjusted values of today's market price. Plenty enough to ensure some lives, he hoped.

With a labored grunt, and his muscle and sinew burning to keep the load secured, he trudged forward bent over and exited the dig site. He plowed onward into the anti-chamber to the left. There was light form above.

He coughed. There was also a lot of smoke. How in God's name could the fire have gotten so close to them in such a short time. Even with the accelerate added by the fuel truck explosion, it should have been longer. They should have had more time.

Ellie appeared. She hung halfway into the hole with her arm out stretched.

"Come on," she urged. "Everybody's out! It's okay!"

Rain put his head down and charged the debris pile. He made it most of the way and fell forward on his knees. Two of the packs unslung from his shoulders. He glanced up at her and froze as Ellie was pulled back from the hole screaming.

Rain tensed and flicked his eyes left to right in rapid succession. He waited to see what was going on and dared not move. Hedger suddenly appeared at the hole and pointed his gun down at him.

"Come on up here," he said, a warning note to his words. "Heave the bags up, crawl out, and don't try anything funny."

Rain heaved both the fallen bags up. He climbed the rest of the way, hauled his weight out of the hole and fell onto his back, with both packs laid at his sides. Hedger backed away and kept the gun on him. Griggs ran over to give a hand keeping the hostages held.

Griggs swept his gun left and right. The frightened hostages cringed back form him and gave strangled cries of fright. Ellie was holding both kids and stood a short distance away. She and Rain locked eyes. As long as they could see each other, it would be okay.

Griggs stood over Rain's prone body as he struggled to breathe easily again. He kept coughing. The smoke was getting to be too much. Griggs smirked at him and brought up a walkie.

"Hey, boss," he began, "we got your Ranger and his tour guide girlfriend. They were escaping with the hostages. Over."

Porter snagged a radio off Dixon's belt and listened. The message came through loud and clear and Porter pumped his fist in the air. His teeth were clinched in a determined snarl.

"Very well," he said. "Where are you?"

"Outside," came Griggs' reply. "They tunneled out pretty close to your dig site by the looks of it."

Porter's smile faltered. He had to check on the status of the gold. What if they grabbed it. He had to go to the hole. Maybe Griggs would know. That's when Griggs came back at him on the walkie.

"We have everybody."

"What about the gold?" Porter asked. "Over."

"The gold too," replied Griggs. "The Ranger had it on him."

Porter grabbed the radio hard and held it against his chest. He closed his eyes tightly and breathed out a long sigh to relax himself. At least it was still safe. That was his only concern. The only reason he would ever travel to some back water hickville like this.

"Good," answered Porter. "We're coming to you."

"Hurry up, sir," said Griggs. "It's starting to get toasty up here."

"Got'cha." said Porter. "We won't be long now."

Porter thrust the radio back at Dixon. The man fumbled with it, then hooked it back on his belt as Porter forged on ahead and they ran to keep up with him.

Rain was sitting up now. He dusted off his hands on his pant legs and stared at Griggs with distaste.

"Do you actually think," began Rain, "that you're gonna make it out of here?"

"I'd bet good money on it." he said, a smug look spread across his ruddy face. He kicked a rucksack of the gold to further illustrate his confident stand. Rain shook his head in chagrin and was getting ready to argue further when they were suddenly interrupted.

"I wouldn't."

That was all that was said. Rain gave a jump. He recognized Tatum's voice before he even set eyes on the man. You don't have to see such an old friend to know who you were listening to. Even if the voice carried the strain of a deep burden.

Before he could get the answers to these questions. Rain had some work to do. Griggs had whirled on the sound of Tatum's voice and turned his back on Rain completely. Hedger had also. Rain saw Griggs was just going to open fire and the hell with it. He knew the body language too well.

He lunged and grabbed onto Griggs at the knees. Rain tugged hard and the man's feet went out from under him. Griggs slammed into the grass chest first and his air was taken form his lungs with a loud POP!

The gun fired and a burst of rounds ripped a chunk out of a pine back behind Tatum. As the weapon skittered out of Griggs' grasp. He was gasping and writhing and bucked like a fish out of water about to suffocate.

Rain got on his knees and rolled the man over, his fist held high about to strike, then realized he didn't need to. Crimson was rapidly staining the flannel over shirt Griggs wore. When he fell, he landed on a sharp chunk of rock, sandstone, which protruded out of the center of his chest. He was gasping for air.

Hedger paused just long enough to give Tatum the opportunity. He was jostling from Rain to Tatum as if he were wondering who was the greater threat. Tatum appeared the easier target and Hedger swung his gun at him.

Tatum brought up the incendiary device he had used to set the backfire and blasted off one of the golf ball shaped explosive pellets. The bomb hit Hedger in the gut and exploded and lifted him into the air.

Hedger the Human Torch flew past the gaping hole and landed, suspended in a pine and burning. His screams died rapidly and soon the rest of the tree was starting to catch fire.

Rain watched him burn and die, then turned his attention briefly to Griggs. He placed a hand over his mouth to check for breath. Tears had streamed from the man's horrified eyes and formed a rug of mud around his head. Rain felt no air and pried away from him.

Rain got to his feet. Ellie separated from the kids and ran to him. She threw herself into him and they embraced. Rain looked past her and tipped his head up at Tatum.

"What are you doing here?" he asked.

"I stuck around," Tatum replied. "Figured you might need me."

Ellie and Rain parted. He touched along the small of her back as she went to tend to the hostages. They were all huddled together, coughing at the thick smoke that steadily began to roll in, thicker and thicker. Rain looked around. It was everywhere like a ghostly vail of fog.

"How did the fire get here so fast?" he asked. Tatum was silent as if he were plotting it in his mind what he wanted to say before he said it. He was careful.

"My backfire," he began, "didn't workout. I thought if I set one it would slow this monster down."

Rain had bent to pick up a rucksack. His fingers had only brushed against one strap when he froze. He glared at Tatum a second and then stood to his full height. His accusatory stare made Tatum drop his head.

"Come on, man," said Rain. "You know not to set a backfire with something like this. It just adds fuel to it."

Tatum only nodded. He still refused to make himself meet Rain's gaze. Ellie was tending to an elderly couple in her group when Tatum and Rain were talking. She paid close attention to their conversation and upon hearing that a backfire was started, she turned her attention to the two men.

"Fire insurance," she said.

Rain perked up. He glanced furtively over at her. "What do you mean?" he asked.

"That's what Porter meant by fire insurance," she said. She met Rain's eyes. "That's what he told me when I wanted to know how he was going to get away. He said he had fire insurance."

Rain looked from her to Tatum and back again a couple of times. Rain turned and strode closer to Tatum. This time Tatum met his friends eyes and his guilt ridden expression said it all.

"Why?" asked Rain.

Before Tatum could respond, a gust of wind blew over the knoll and a pyroclast of ash and cinders permeated their area. The hostages began to scatter and flail at themselves and the hair and clothes, afraid they were all going to catch fire.

"I did what I did because I needed money," he said. "I'm in trouble."

"More that you know," replied Rain.

The wind picked up again and a fresh burst of cinders floated through the air around them. Ellie tried to get everybody to group together again. Sweat was rolling off everyone's foreheads now. The heat was rising more and more by the minute.

"I don't think we have time to debate this," Tatum said.

Rain was thinking back, not a couple of months ago, he and Tatum were on their kayaks and headed down river on one of their recreational treks they took form time to time.

He remembered Tatum had mentioned he was having trouble paying the rent on the house he was staying in. With his wife's passing two years back, that left him paying for it all and the landlord wouldn't let him do odd jobs around the place to get a little knocked off the price.

They both had debts. He had told Rain she especially had quite a lot of credit card charges and he was also trying to pay these off. Now that he thought back on it, Tatum was troubled for a long time.

Conversations that used to come easy had begun to be stilted and the fun time the two best friends shared wasn't quite as fun. Tatum always seemed to be somewhere else, even when Rain did something with him that Tatum loved to do.

That's why they took the little boats out. Rain loved exercise as much as the next person, but to him the kayaks were brutal torture devices he could do with out. He had agreed to do it for Tatum. After his hinting at how bad things were for him, Tatum had seemed better. Somewhat. Now this.

"Second chance time," said Rain. "Good deeds to erase bad ones."

Tatum shook his head. "I broke all the rules. Tom."

"We're fighting fire with fire here," said Rain, "when you do that...there are no rules."

Rain glared at him. Tatum nodded. He took in a deep breath and slowly let it out.

"What can I do?"

"Get these people to the visitor center," said Rain. "Try to call for help."

Tatum forced a smile. Rain nodded slightly at him at return, then shifted his stance so suddenly he nearly lost footing. From below them, Rain heard an audible CLICK and knew the sound of a safety being switch off on a weapon.

A burst of gunfire drove Rain back off the rim of the hole. Tatum tossed the flair gun to him. Rain caught it and ran up on the lip of the hole. He looked down and locked eyes with Porter. Before he could finish loading in a fresh clip, Rain fired three of the explosive balls down at them.

"Get down!" screamed Porter. He shoved Holland out of the way. Cates and Dixon dove behind a large rock and Porter hurled himself back into the anti-chamber. The incendiary devices exploded on contact with the cave floor.

The explosion caved in more of the ceiling and sealed the exit hole again. The fire blew out and Porter stared in disbelief and the smoldering new pile of debris that blocked the way.

"God damn it!" he raged.

"Now we have to get out the way we came in," said Cates.

"By that time, they'll be long gone on foot," added Dixon.

Porter couldn't believe this. What was going on here? He found himself out witted at every turn, it seemed, by a forest ranger and a tour guide.

They were resourceful. He could give them that. He would just let his anger take control. When he did that, he could be pretty resourceful himself.

"Now what?" asked Holland as he dusted himself off. Cates and Dixon shouldered weapons and awaited the order from Porter.

"Get the dirt bikes out of the vans," began Porter. "Then we track them. We'll have them in no time."

CHAPTER 11

ON THE MOVE

Rain tossed the weapon down. He knelt and started to shoulder the bags. Ellie came over to help and gave Tatum a disapproving stare as she crossed in front of him. She hefted a sack and got it firmly on the middle of her back.

Rain pulled on two of the rucksacks and helped Ellie with the other one. The wind kicked up a notch and the roar of the approaching fire carried to them. He called to Tatum.

"You better get going."

Tatum nodded. He helped an elderly couple get up from the ground and gave Rain and Ellie the most apologetic look he could muster at the moment. Ellie's facade refused to soften.

Tatum began leading the way down the trail to get back to the center. Rain watched after him for a moment as he took point.

"This way everybody," called Tatum, "stay together and follow me."

Rain looked Ellie over and opened his mouth to say something. She knew he was planning to talk her out of helping and she wasn't going to hear it. She cut him off before he could even begin to start up.

"I'm going with you," she stated emphatically. "You can't talk me out of it, so let's get going." Rain smirked.

"Are you sure you can make it?"

"Yeah," she said and indicated the bag with a tilt of her head. "It's not bad. Where are we going?"

"To the Falling Waters side," said Rain. "We gotta hide this stuff."

Ellie looked around at their surroundings. She noted the wall of fire that darkened the hillsides and bathed all the land in a deep orange hue. They were pinned in with no evident way to get out.

"We're going to need horses," she said.

"We still have some?" asked Rain.

"Yeah. The equestrian facilities haven't been cleared yet." she replied. "Only we have to go through that."

She pointed to the wall of flames. Rain glanced around them. "Maybe we can find away around," he said. "Come on."

They started down from the mound and crossed the trail Tatum took the hostages down. They moved down into the thickets, headed out across country.

Porter drove one of the dirt bikes down a steel ramp and onto the parking lot. Holland got on and rolled out behind him. They waited.

Dixon and Cates emerged out of the covered trailer next to them on one more. Holland tapped Porter on the arm as they prepared to start out and pointed up at the visitor center.

Tatum was peering down at them. Porter followed his arm and spotted him. Holland watched Tatum as he glanced furtively their way and motioned the hostages into the building.

"What about them?" asked Holland.

"Fuck the lot of 'em!" snapped Porter. "They can do whatever they want. All that matters is the fucking gold."

Porter kick started his bike. Tatum stared back at them as he waved the last hostages into the shelter of the visitor center gift shop. Porter gave him the finger and pulled away. His back tire burned a half circle mark on the pavement.

Dixon and Cates exchanged a look of uncertainty about their situation. They were getting ready to drive right into the brunt of the blaze after all. Dixon and Cates kick started their bikes as well and fish tailed out after Porter.

Out in the depth of the burning woods, the crew chief and his whipped men and women were still trying to stop the tide of fire.

Hoses were advanced and pulled back in a desperate dance. All involved were near to heat exhaustion, if not all out stroke.

Dugger heaved his way over to Chief Bradley. He had collapsed earlier and was wrapped in a white towel that was soaked with water. He had it around his neck and shoulders.

Against intense heat like this, it only kept you cool for no more than a few minutes, but at least it was something. Bradley turned to him. He put an arm gently on his shoulder.

"You look whipped my friend!"

"I'm good," replied Dugger. "How are we doing?"

Bradley watched as his crew advanced on the blaze yet again and unleashed four hoses at high power. The teams were nearly thrown off their feet by the force. The fire receded and then reared back at them.

"Maybe we can hold off till the dumpers come."

"How far out are they?" asked Dugger

"Last word," replied Bradley, "about forty minutes more."

Dugger shook his head. He started for one of the hose teams, to spell one of the others. They all looked to him to be in worse shape. Bradley made to hold him back. Dugger shrugged him off and waved off any help.

"Said I was cool."

"Not for long!"

Dugger raised his left hand into the air and closed his fingers to his thumb to make a "shut your mouth" sign. Bradley smirked.

"All right," he began. "I'll shut up. But when you stroke out don't come cryin' to me!"

The rescued wiped tears, sweat, and grime from their faces with towels. Tatum handed out the last one he had on his arm to Sue and Robbie.

Tatum went to the wall behind the counter and managed to reach the thermostat. The air was running, but considering the condition they found themselves in at the moment, it did little to nothing to cut out the heat.

He turned it down a few more degrees. He shrugged. If the unit quit running, so what. The fire was closing on them anyway. If they were all going to burn up eventually, he thought they might as well throw caution to the wind.

He came back out in front of his weary crowd and stood before them. He pointed a group of people to the drink coolers.

"There's water and sodas there," he said.

"There's ice cream in the little freezer. Help yourselves."

Tourists started taking sodas and waters greedily and knocked over a snack display. Tatum scowled at them.

"Careful!" he yelled. "There's plenty to go around!"

Sue and Robbie squeezed themselves out from between the legs of the pushing and shoving throng, and came up to Tatum.

"What now?" she asked.

"Just try to take it easy," he said. "We're okay for now. I'm going to call out and try to get us some help."

He patted her on the arm and she smiled at him. Tatum turned away and crossed to the counter again. The C.B. Radio was there and probably was their only safe bet. The phones were certain to not be working by now.

He kept thinking of Ellie and how she had looked at him, even after he saved them, and the smile the little girl just gave him. How could he have helped these men do this?

Nothing was worth losing your dignity. No amount of money could buy that back. Once it was gone, it was a long and painful way to get it back. He realized that now.

He fought back tears and had to fumble around under the counter before his vision cleared and his hands found the old radio. He pulled it out and sat it on the counter. He picked up the mike and took in a breath to steady himself for what he had to do.

"This is..." he began, not sure how he should address himself to listeners and he nodded to himself to affirm what he wanted to say.

"This is Forest Ranger John Tatum," he began.

"Calling from the Marietta Caverns Park. I have fourteen people with me at the visitor center and we need evacuation!"

He paused to let that register and to collect his thoughts. He took in another breath and continued, "If anyone can hear me, please respond."

He waits a few moments. Sue and Robbie were watching him intently. Robbie nodded to him to let him know he was doing fine. Tatum gave a thumbs up and continued his hail.

"Say again," he began. "This is forest ranger John Tatum..."

Dugger and Bradley were outside their makeshift command center, a large green military style tent haphazardly yanked over a bunch of poles, and were headed back out to the crews, when Tatum's message crackled out of their radio set.

They exchanged bewildered looks and trudged back into the tent. They waited to hear anything else and at that moment Tatum began his second hail. Bradley slapped his thigh with his dusty hat.

"What?" demanded Dugger.

"That dumb ass ranger!" he yelled. "If he hadn't set that goddamn backfire we wouldn't be in near this much shit!"

Dugger frowned at the indignant stand his leader took. He glanced from the chief to the radio and back again.

"What do we do?" he asked. "Try to find a way through?"

Bradley waved his arms and shook his head wildly. He was angered that Dugger even suggest sparing any men to go to their aid especially when he felt that Tatum was entirely in the wrong.

"No, no,no!" he vehemently said. "We need everybody we got right here if we're gonna ride this out until the dumpers come."

"What about them?" asked Dugger, incredulously.

"The ranger can cover it," said Bradley. "We have to keep the fire at bay."

Bradley gave Dugger a warning glance not to push the issue with him. Bradley turned and slung out of the tent. Dugger frowned and followed after him. His anger was about to boil over.

He found it difficult to contain himself in his own skin.

He strode up next to Bradley and fell into pace with him. He leaned his head down close to the man's ear.

"When we get out of this," he said. "I'm going to see to it you're removed as chief."

Bradley scowled at him. He tried to be angry but he was also hurt that a man he considered a friend, even though he was an employee, would turn on him this way because of that ranger.

"You do what you have to," said Bradley. He moved off toward one of the hose teams. "And I'll do what I have to."

Dugger stood there a moment and glared at Bradley's back. Then he continued on toward another team that waged war with the beast in the distance.

Rain and Ellie had covered a pretty good amount of ground in a very short time. They had to be more than a mile from the knoll and were rapidly covering the rough terrain despite their heavy loads.

The smoke forced barking coughs from their mouths at times and the heat was causing them to be bathed in their own sweat. They had tried two different paths and found themselves cut off by walls of burning bushes and trees.

They were forced to head to higher and higher ground to try and get around the blaze as it ran uphill. That's just what fire did. That was it's natural law. And that's what they battled. Perhaps they would be trapped here. They were going against nature now.

They trudged through sloughs of dried leaves, nearly to their hips in certain spots, and drove striped lizards and toads from their dry hiding places.

Rain's mind raced as they pushed themselves onward. He ignored his own body's cries of protest under the weight of the gold as they climbed a hill, over nature's staircase of tangled roots and granite pieces.

He thought about Tatum. They should have made it to the visitor center a while ago, and with any luck, maybe the hostages would be all right until help could come to them.

Rain heard two tragic tales of life's unfairness today. First, it was Johnny who sold away his heritage and then it was Tatum who sold away his beliefs. Two friends that he should have tried better to help along the way.

Rain knew that Tatum was having trouble. But, then again, Rain had his own problems to deal with. That's just the way it is. When you're able to offer help, nobody needs or wants it. But when you can't help, then people seem to need you most. Rain and Ellie had been together a long time and he was fighting to hold onto their life together.

He turned this all over as they distanced themselves form the park and the men who would be following soon. He tried to keep an ear open to Ellie as he let his brain run on overdrive. He heard a labored grunt that was new and sounded pained, but not enough to stop him.

"You all right?" he asked.

"I'm good," was all she said. It was enough to let him know that she was not good at all right now. Rain put on the brakes and turned to her.

He extended his arm and side stepped back toward her but she was going down. She fell onto her side, lost the packs in the process, and lay there panting. Rain ran back to her and got down on one knee.

"I'm sorry," he said, about not catching her in time.

"I was thinking."

"About Tatum?" she asked. He nodded. "I can't believe he helped them do this."

Rain reached out his hand. She clamped onto his forearm as well and he pulled her to her feet. She kept her hands on her knees and breathed a little easier. He stroked her back with the tips of his fingers.

"That's not all," he said. "You know Johnny Two-Feathers?"

"Yeah." she said. Then a revelation came to her. "Yeah. I think he was on the tour but I was so distracted I couldn't be sure," Rain nodded.

"He was." Ellie stood up and she locked eyes with Rain. "He told them where the gold was, and it was his family's."

Ellie dropped her hands and they clapped against her thighs. "That surprises me," she said. "Though it shouldn't, as tough as times are."

Rain was about to reply when a long CREAKING sound and a SNAP that was loud as pounding thunder filled their ears. They were stopped near a rock that jutted from the ground and had to step around this to see.

Then they saw the big oak tree fall. They heard it as well with it's heavy thudding as it laid waste to the ground around it and every small tree and fallen log unlucky enough to exist beneath its boughs. The fire had finally claimed it, the ring of fire was no match for it's bulk either. The force of it's impact blew away part of the raging flames and left a hole big enough to drive several cars through. Nature battled nature here.

The tree ended up across the line of fire and provided the break through that Rain and Ellie had hoped for. Ellie squealed with delight at the sight of it. Rain glanced after and couldn't help but smile a little himself.

"Why did you come back?" she asked suddenly. Rain was sort of shocked by her directness and the time she chose to ask. Now wasn't the time or place to tell the truth so he had to get them moving. Blosion was best for now.

"I know you guys would need help," he said. "When the fire jumped the road, I thought I could do something."

She walked back over to where her rucksacks lay on the ground and started pulling herself into one. Rain came to her and held the other one until she got ready to take it. She knew he was avoiding her question, yet she still grinned.

"I bet you didn't expect all this, huh?"

"No," Rain admitted and smiled back. "No, I didn't."

The smile was wiped from Rain's lips in an instant. Ellie turned her head in all directions, looking. The sound of the dirt bikes came to them from the distance. They were mobile and they were searching.

Rain gritted his teeth. They were sure to catch up to them soon. He had hoped they would be on foot. He knew they would come but he never expected them to have bikes. That may just give them the edge out here, even as well as Rain knew this territory.

Rain handed Ellie the other sack. She hurried to get it up on her shoulders. Rain hitched up his own packs and spared another quick glance back the way they came.

"Let's move." He led them out, headed toward the fallen tree. Fire had already crept back up around it and threatened to close off the gap. Ellie darted to catch up to him.

Griggs rolled violently onto his side as his whole body spasmed. He groped at his burning chest and coughed several harsh, deep coughs as he struggled for air amid the smoke.

He held a hand to his chest and pressed around, like a blind man that felt his way, and found the piece of sandstone lodged in the center of it. It had missed his heart and missed his lungs. It was still wedged in the soft tissue fairly deep.

When that ranger dragged him off his feet, he landed hard. He groped the piece of rock with both hands and tugged as hard as he could to free it.

He shut his eyes tight and groaned through clenched teeth as he yanked it free. A gout of blood splashed onto his hands and the dirt. He rolled over and that's when he saw what remained of Hedger.

Griggs pitched up and vomited all over the ground. Then he lay back on his side and tried not to look. He managed to tear a ragged strip of his shirt off and packed it into the open wound with his finger.

"Aw, Christ," he swore.

Griggs got his feet gingerly. He kept his hands on his knees and got his breathing under control. He grabbed for his empty gun and pulled it up by the strap and cradled it in his hands.

He heard the dirt bikes as they came toward him on the trail. He stumbled that way. He trudged out onto the path and waved his arms. Porter and Holland stopped their bikes next to him. Cates and Dixon parked and idled a short distance behind.

"We thought you guys were dead," said Porter.

"Hedger is."

"Can you ride?"

Porter was eyeing the bloody rag stuffed into the man's chest with curiosity. Griggs suddenly got the feeling that if he didn't say he was close as could be to one hundred percent that Porter would finish him off right now.

"Yeah," said Griggs. He tried to sound confident. "Not a problem."

Porter gave him an odd little smile that suggested he knew better but had no time to argue the point. So he would humor Griggs.

"Get on with Holland then." he said. There was barely any room. Griggs got on behind Holland. He handed Griggs a clip for his gun which he took and slammed into the bay. Then they were off to chase after Porter.

CHAPTER 12

YOU DON'T SEE
THAT EVERY DAY

Rain pushed aside a smoldering limb and it snapped off. He crushed some twigs underfoot and wiped the ashes off on his pant's legs. He had made it onto the obstacle course of the fallen tree.

Careful not to get too near the fire that had now begun to devour the remains, he reached out for Ellie, and shielded himself from the heat with his free arm. She grabbed on, and he pulled her up with him.

She looked past his upper body. Rain glanced back at her. They shared a look of concern. Rain edged out a little from her and extended a hand which she took.

"Come on," he said. "Hold tight." She nodded and got her feet moving. Rain led the way. He hurried but tried to be as careful as possible with his footing. He made an effort to dig into the bark with his boot and glanced back at her, indicating where the good foothold was.

The swung over a dead limb that reached for the darkened sky as if it wanted to claw the heavens. They came out on the other side of the fire break into a literal ring of fire. They were now in the eye of Hell's own hurricane.

Rain hadn't planned on this. He grimaced as he took in the view. He knew conditions were unstable in something like this. They had to move fast and find a way out. Hopefully soon.

Ellie stared around in disbelief. She thought, if they made it past the firewall, they would be home free. The buildings for the equestrian facility were beyond the other side. Past the second wall of flames.

"Oh, my God," she whispered.

Rain helped her down to the ground. He started forward, grunting under the weight of the bags. Ellie groaned with exhaustion and trailed after him. She felt like she was ready to drop dead.

They were about a hundred yards into the clearing when she was wracked by a fit of coughs. She barked them out, face deep red, and Rain turned and ran back for her. She looked like she was choking. He put a hand on her shoulder to steady her.

"Are you okay?" he asked. Ellie nodded and got control enough to reply.

"It's just getting hard to breathe!"

Rain tore a strip off his torn pants and tied it around her head to cover her nose and mouth.

"Breath through with your mouth," he said.

He breathed with her, nodded his head, and she nodded back. It was working. She could breath a little better. She took several deeper breaths.

"Okay?" he asked.

She nodded. Rain continued on. He charged ahead and glanced back. Ellie hopped over a fallen limb and kept up.

"We have to hurry," he said. "It's dangerous in here."

"Not much farther now," she managed. She was going to say more and them a bewildered look came over her face and she froze. Rain stopped moving and turned to her. He was about to ask her what was wrong when he heard a familiar noise. A dreaded noise, and he knew.

The sky began to get darker and darker as the wind picked up to a deafening roar and all the smoke was pulled into a dome above the ring of fire.

The flames all around them surged and climbed higher due to the influx of air. Tendrils of bright orange fire separated from one side of the wall. They lashed out like whips into the open air.

The wind continued to roar and swept down into the clearing between the firewalls. Tendrils of fire began to lash out again, rapidly, like lighting strikes and began to merge into bigger shapes and formed funnels, that twisted and turned in midair.

Rain and Ellie watched it all happen. Ellie reached up and felt the back of her neck. The hairs there stood on end like being in a lighting storm. Rain shuddered the length of his body. He felt it too.

The swirling tendrils of fire spread into the air almost reaching the top of the smoke dome and their tips flirted with the dry ground. Sparks jumped and flashed under the heat and began to ignite the wire grass clusters nearby.

The wind seared down into the makeshift valley created by the walls of fire and drove the bright orange twisters onto the earth with such force that the burning wire grass was blasted into ash clouds.

Rain glanced rapidly all around them. He spotted several more beech trees in the distance, off to there right. It was their only chance. They had to cover about two hundred yards. They nodded to each other and broke into a run.

Rain grunted and spat as his powerful legs dug into the ground. He charged as hard as the weight he carried would allow. Ellie labored to keep up and stayed right on his heels.

The fire tornadoes twisted and lashed across the ground where they had formed as the wind pumped its fuel into them. They howled as they churned and churned gaining power. They burned brighter and grew larger, almost white hot.

The firewall separated from them and the tendrils of flame broke off. The fire tornadoes were fully formed. They plowed the ground, back and forth and all around, burning the earth. They seemed to move as if they were hunters that searched for prospective prey.

Rain spared a glance that way. There were three of them. He gave a defiant roar and hurtled himself further ahead. Ellie groaned as her weaker legs strained to keep pace.

She looked past him. The trees were closer. Close enough to hope for. The wind was now pelting them with blades of grass, dirt particles, and leaves.

The tornadoes spread out form their start up point and zigzagged across the path way of each other as they burned the mark upon the ground and headed straight toward Rain and Ellie. It was just a question of which team would reach the stand of breech trees first.

Rain and Ellie shielded their faces with the forearm and ran nearly bent over as the wind from the advancing tornadoes bore down on them. The tornadoes crossed paths once more and then again, and two formed into one.

They plowed into the other side of the breech grove and began to blast the smaller trees into debris. A limb was hurled at them. It's flaming girth nearly flatted Ellie. She hit the ground an instant before it got there.

The limb crashed into the ground a few feet past her head and sat the grasses afire. Rain had spotted cover and bent to pull her to it. She kicked with her feet as he dragged her.

"Get up!" he yelled. "Come with me!"

"I'm trying!"

He dragged her up and she got her feet planted underneath her. They looked up to see the third tornado whipsaw through the debris and merge with the other two.

The surge of power was immense. A heatwave burned into Rain and Ellie. She screamed and flailed with her arms to block it. Rain shut his eyes tight and hooked an arm around her waist.

He surged to his left and they cantered into an opening in the massive trunk of the largest beech tree.

There was just enough room for them to stay crouched on their knees.

The three tornadoes were now one massive twister of demon breath. The wind picked up to it's highest gust and drove the spinning desecrater in.

The smallest trees splintered and caught fire in midair. Flaming, smoking debris whirled all around the twister and obliterated the rest of the small ones of the groves.

The twister lept forward and ripped large trees in half. Their parts were felled all around the big tree. Ellie screamed and Rain held her close as the massive old tree vibrated and violently shuddered. The twister was trying to tear it apart to get them.

"It's okay!" roared Rain. "It's all right!"

"No!" screamed Ellie.

"You're okay!"

The twister passed over the tree. Rain glanced out the opening. They were literally inside the funnel. The twister sat there and small bits of detritus fell on them as the tree shook. It felt as if they were the rag doll in the hands of an angry child.

Rain pulled back, he and Ellie shrunk as far as they could inside the tree. He didn't even dare to breathe. The fire in the opening licked and reached a little ways into the hole as if it searched for them. Like it tried to see if it could feel them and grab them in it's clutches.

The shaking abruptly stopped. The twister fully passed over them and was angrily spinning out across the clearing toward where Rain and Ellie came in.

Rain breathed out a tremendous sigh. He was holding his breath a long time and now he took in several rapid gulps of air. Ellie did too. They hauled themselves out of the tree trunk and took advantage of the clean air around them.

They watched the tornado. It was dissipating. The wind had begun to die down. The smoke was now descending back into the area and would then choke them as they battled their way across. Rain looked at the remains of the beech grove.

All that stood was the entre trunk of their big tree and two half trunks of a couple trees that were slighty larger than the rest. Everything else had been reduced to graying coals.

"You don't see that everyday," said Rain.

Ellie tried to laugh but it broke down into another round of coughs.

"We better go," he said. He squeezed her shoulder. She smiled just before she pulled her mask over her nose and mouth.

Porter stopped his bike. He looked closely at the fire break where the wall of fire stood unbroken. It was burning up. Porter reached into his bag and pulled out a map of the grounds. Holland and Griggs looked on. He glanced up at them.

"Got this," he began, "from the visitor center. Thought it might come in handy."

"Where can they be?" asked Holland.

"If they can make it through this firewall," he said, "the horseback riding facility is there."

He tapped the upper right comer of the map with two fingers. Porter smiled.

"From there, he's got no choice but to go to Falling Waters. Which is just what I want."

Cates and Dixon exchanged bewildered looks. Porter only cackled and tucked his map away.

"All is not lost," he said. "You see?"

Just then, the remnants of the twisters blew through the firewall, and punched some serious gaps in it which reformed instantly into the wall.

The super heated air rushed across the ground at them, tossed drifts of leaves into the air, and nearly tossed them from their bikes.

Holland struggled to keep himself upright. The fact that Griggs was acting like he couldn't support himself didn't help matters. Cates and Dixon shielded their faces from debris.

The remains of the fire tornadoes died away. The swirling clouds of leaves and debris fell to the ground. They now were looking around, unsure of what just happened.

"What the hell was that?" asked Porter.

He checked the faces of all his men. They were just as confused as he was about what just happened. The gusty winds had now died and all was still. He glances around again, and spotted something in the distance, that interested him. He looked almost hopeful in his eyes.

"Come on," he said, "Let's keep going!"

Porter started his bike and pulled away. His back wheel spread out a rooster tail of dirt and the others watched him travel on. They shared an irritated look and followed on.

Tatum was still sweating over the radio. All the people were drenched in sweat and they were going through drinks in the cooler at a good clip, soon they would be out. Tatum checked the air. He had it turned as low as he dared go and it did nothing to cut the heat.

He watched them. As he did, he thought about what he would do if they got out of this mess.

Would he turn himself in and come clean about his involvement? People had been killed up here. For what? So he could make his life easier. He hated himself more every time he thought about it.

He forced a smile at Robbie and Sue as they sipped Pepsi and glanced over at him. He decided the past would be taken care of in due time. What mattered most was right now. He decided to try the radio again.

"This is forest ranger John Tatum at Marietta Caverns," he began. "I have tourists that need evacuation. We need assistance. The fire is almost on us. Somebody help us!"

He puts his head on his wrist and closed his eyes. Tears had begun to roll down his face and pool on the ground as he thought all hope to be gone. The the radio crackled and a voice came through. It was the voice of the dump plane pilot.

"This is Rick Conners," he said. "of Red Bay One. We're getting ready to dump some water for you guys. See if we can't put it out."

Tatum pumped his fist in the air. The crowd burst into loud cheers and applause. The radio crackled again and they all fell silent.

"We'll be there in about fifteen minutes," he said. "Over."

"Copy that!" replied Tatum. "We'll hold on! Thank you!"

More cheers went up from within the crowd. Tatum pounded the counter with his fist in rapid succession and finally does break down in relief.

Sue came over and rubbed at his upper arm. Robbie was with her. Tatum got himself under control and smiled down at her. Robbie gave him a thumbs up.

"You did it," he said. "Way to go."

Tatum grinned. He returned the thumbs up gesture. He was amazed. He had always heard that children could be cruel. He also realized that children can be more caring than adults ever could when they chose to.

CHAPTER 13

A STICKY END

Rain and Ellie were out in the open now. They were charging hard as they could muster, weighed down as they were, and had covered the last of the open field. Now they were cutting their way over rough ground and they darted through small thickets of tiny trees and their choking under growth.

Rain coughed hard, barked out several jagged ones, and Ellie clubbed him on the back to help. The flaming small trees did little more than make thick smoke that permeated what clean air they had and the acridness and dryness of it was what stifled them both the most.

Rain cursed Tatum in his mind. Damn him for doing this. How could he have helped those men?

Rain still couldn't wrap his mind around why. It was simply inconceivable.

Then his thoughts turned to the hostages at the park as he and Ellie scrambled around another brush clump and through thick wiregrass where flame nipped hungrily at their heels. He hoped they would make it and be able to ride out the firestorm there.

Ellie groaned as one of her packs slipped from her shoulders and threatened to pull her down with it. Rain turned and charged back to her. He helped her get her arm unwound from the bag straps and they stood there panting.

She gave a little laugh at their situation. Here they were, brought back together by a desperate set of circumstances and on the run from bad guys with a fortune in lost gold. It was too much like a silly treasure hunt movie for her. She had to laugh a little at the absurdity or she would break down.

"What's the matter," asked Rain. He was looking her over with the kind of careful observation she had come to despise lately and she felt the familiar surge in her blood that came before anger rose in her. She tried to suppress it. He was only concerned. She had to tell herself that.

Rain was always that way. He was a mother hen their entire time together. He would ask and ask until you got so tired of saying you were okay, swearing that you were indeed fine, that nothing was wrong at all-until you finally had to snap his head off for not letting go. She used to love it, even though she got annoyed with it. She would try to overlook it like she used to. She just shook her head.

"Just overwhelmed," she said. "I can't believe what we're in the middle of here."

Rain nodded. He grabbed her by the shoulders and squeezed gently. He kissed her very softly and pulled himself back to appraise her. This time the mother hen concern was gone. He knew she was okay and that she could do this. He simply admired her a moment. He started to speak, but his ears had pricked up at the faint sound of the off road bikes coming closer. They had to be on the other side of the firewall.

"What?" asked Ellie. He shushed her and when she started to speak again, he gently placed his finger tips over her lips to silence her.

"Listen," he said. She strained her ears, listened hard and she raised her eyebrows. "Can you hear'em?"

"Yeah," she said. "Now I can. They're closer than before."

She looked around frantic to find cover. Rain joined her in the search. "If they break through," she began. "They'll be on top of us in no time flat!"

"I know," said Rain. He searched wildly, whirled around this way and that, and stepped away to the left. He saw a rabbit trail between wafts of smoke. He remembered that it led to some shelter. They might be able to hide until they can form a plan.

"Over there!" he said, and pointed. Ellie nodded and clapped him on the shoulder blade. He reached down and grabbed her pack. He helped her shoulder it and spared a quick glance at the firewall on the far side of the clearing.

Porter stopped his bike. His men drove up and pulled in alongside him. He pointed to the downed tree that stretched it's wide girth across the firebreak. Flames flicked and flashed across the top of it, but it could provide the way through.

"We can get through there," yelled Porter.

"How exactly," said Cates. "Jump?"

"Precisely," stated Porter.

He gunned the engine and slung the bike around, cutting a deep groove in the ground and threw hot dirt into the air all around them. He rode up onto a hill to get a good straight angle at the base of the tree where the earth was mounded for a ramp.

Cates turned his own bike and snuck watchful glances at Porter. He waited to see whether their boss's latest half baked idea was going to work. He couldn't wait to be shed of him once this was over and he was certain the others felt the same. One glance at Dixon's strained features told him so.

Porter checked behind him to see that they were following. He waved his arm forward and pointed at the base of the tree. Cates nodded in return and Porter was off.

Porter's face was a mask of concentration as he sped toward his jumping off point. He clenched his teeth and tried to shut out the scream of fear that came from Griggs. For the man to be so near death he certainly had good voice and a better grip. Holland felt like the man behind him was going to squeeze his lungs out.

Porter turned the wheel right over so slightly and locked his arms as he braced for impact and gripped the handle bar white knuckle tight.

Porter's bike hit the dip in the embankment and went airborn. They rose up, narrowly avoided limbs, and the back tire shredded bark off the toasted tree. Porter stood and pulled up with both arms to try and elevate the bike a little more, considering the extra weight. They went higher as flames licked at the wheels and plunged down into the grasslands on the other side.

The bike bounced twice upon landing and Griggs tried to grasp Holland's flailing arms to try and keep the man from falling. He couldn't. The impacts were jarring and Holland was plucked from between himself and Porter, then thrown nearly thirty feet, where he landed on his neck and lay still. Porter grimaced. He knew there was no way to help. They just circled around to watch. He had heard the thud of Cates' bike as it dug in to make the leap.

Porter threw his head back as he saw the bike erupt over the end of the tree and punch through a tongue of smoke and flame. Cates crashed down hard, bounced, and both men were nearly thrown. He got control and wrested the bike around to stop short of Porter by a few feet.

"Oh, my God," whispered Ellie. They had watched the whole thing take place. She whipped her head around to look at Rain. Rain nodded in agreement with her exaltation. He grabbed her by the elbow and pulled her with him.

"We gotta hide," he said. "Come on." Rain hauled her away with him, through a row of scrub brush, and headed for the rabbit trail he pointed out to her earlier.

He ran ahead and stayed low with the sparse cover of the trees around them. Ellie did the same. He hoped against all hope that their thin gray smoke screen would hide them just a moment longer.

Rain pushed aside a small oak tree about his height that stood sentry to the trail and edged past it with Ellie right at his heels. He started down sideways, and kept his feet on the worn path, because the slope fell away sharply into a gully.

Rain led them down and around the hillside and they came out in front of a dark groove in the earth where a large weathered sandstone face jutted out above it. It was a cave, one of many that the native people of the region took refuge in, so many years past.

"Let's go!" he called. He ran on ahead and dropped down to a crouch to enter the shelter of the cave. He reached out to Ellie and locked onto her forearm. He pulled her down with him into the opening. They stripped off their packs and waited.

They panted and tried hard to control their breathing so that they wouldn't call attention to themselves. As they settled down they were able to listen for any sounds of approach. They heard the bikes rev as the men raced in their direction.

"They won't find us here will they?"

"I don't think so," said Rain. "They'll be going too fast. I almost didn't see it and we're on foot."

Rain gripped her by the shoulders and held her tightly against him as the bikes approached. Their rattling, rumbling engines grew louder and he could hear Porter's voice above the din of the motors.

"Go that way!" he called.

"Check over there!" came Dixon's reply.

Ellie turned her head right and left as they heard the bikes go their separate routes. They exchanged looks of relief but continued to hold fast. The motor sounds grew faint for a time, then doubled back toward them.

Ellie started to peer out of the cave, but Rain held her back. She shot him a defiant look and he just shook his head and pointed upward. Up above them, one of the bikes had stopped and sat idling.

Gravels and loose dirt particles fell past them from the lip of the sandstone outcropping. The bike was soon joined by the other one and the motors were shut off. Ellie and rain exchanged looks of apprehension and strained to listen intently.

"Now what?" inquired Cates.

"They're not far," replied Porter. "Keep hunting. We know they're going for the horses."

"What if they're already there?" asked Dixon.

"They're not!" said Porter hotly. "We're right on top of them. I know it."

They heard a bike get throttled up and the driver as he yelled his caveat at Porter before pulling away.

"They better be!" yelled Cates. More detritus fell past them at the opening of the cave as Cates drove angrily away.

"Fucking wankers," snarled Porter.

Porter stood straddled over the bike. Griggs was feebly holding onto him. Porter merely glared after Cates and Dixon's backs as they rode away and their bike disappeared under a thick veil of black smoke.

How he couldn't wait to be shed of this ridiculous crew of people. They get duped repeatedly by a forest ranger and some tour guides, lose the gold to them in the process, and then have the gall to make threats to him?

He fantasized briefly about handing Dixon and Cates their shares and then shooting them center mass in the chest. He was beginning to relish their twin looks of shock and dismay when he was snapped out of his reverie by a whimper from behind him.

"What do we do now?" asked Griggs. He wheezed when he spoke and began to cough. The thickly congested sound told Porter all he needed to know. There was blood in the man's lungs. Porter drew his nickel plated .45 from inside his coat.

"First," he began, "we need to drop some dead weight." He then turned half way around and stuck the nose of the gun under Griggs's ribcage. He fired twice.

Griggs gasped and blood mist burst from between his open lips as the slugs first tore through each of his compromised lungs and then ripped his heart to pieces. He was thrown from the bike and landed hard. Porter watched as the body began to roll over the edge of the hill and gunned his engine. He pulled away, back tire throwing a rut of dirt, and never looked back.

A shower of dirt and rock fell past them as they peered out from under the entrance to the cave. At that instant, Griggs's body dropped down and hung suspended before them, and Ellie screamed.

Rain covered her mouth and winced as she turned away and berried her head in his collar bone. Rain checked her and glanced back at the body that hung in front of them.

"Probably caught on a root," Thought Rain.

He grabbed his packs and hauled them out from under the shelter. He was right. The body was caught. He shouldered the packs. Ellie was coming. She edged herself out to avoid the body and Rain helped her get her packs back on.

"What are we gonna do?" she asked.

"You go on ahead to the stables," said Rain. "I'll distract the other two."

"What about Porter?"

"Stay low," he began. "You know these woods well... and I taught you to hide in them, right?" She nodded. "Once I deal with them, I'll catch up with you."

He kissed her once more and moved past her. He deftly hauled himself up despite the weight on his back and in seconds, stood atop the rise. She waved to him.

"Good luck," she said.

"You too." And with that, he was gone. Ellie waited a moment, hoping for another glimpse of him. When there was none, she rounded the hillside and took the rabbit trail they had used to get down.

Rain was well on his way through the dense trees. The tree cover here was the thickest of all the park grounds. The forest got denser and denser the closer to the Falling Waters section you traveled.

Right now, he was following alongside the horse trail that wound through the pines and birches. The fire blazed on all sides and sweat poured from him and soaked his uniform yet again out of the frying pan, into the fire, and then the blast furnace.

He crouched down by an old moss covered log to get his bearings and figure out his moves. Ahead of him lay a glade that led into a thicket of flaming pines. He heard the engine rattle as the bike neared his position. It was now or never.

Rain broke from his cover and darted onto the open path. Cates rounded the trail up ahead and stopped the bike. They stared each other down. Cates was practically salivating at the deer in headlights expression on the ranger's face.

Rain feigned an attempt to go back the way he came, but ran forward and darted right, headed for the glade. Cates brought the bike up on one wheel as he gave it full throttle and bore down on the spot where Rain was.

Cates couldn't believe their luck. In his haste to retreat, the ranger had dropped one of the rucksacks. He bent to grab the bag and pulled it onto his shoulders.

Dixon clapped him on the back as he watched Rain cross into the glade. Rain spared a quick glance back at them and continued to run away. Dixon shook his head. For a forest ranger, the man was incredibly stupid. He was headed into the mouth of the blaze now, right for the pines, where he would be roasted. He was confident they would get him first. He still had more gold afterall.

"Go after him," said Cates. "I'll circle around and flush him back to you."

Dixon hopped off and slung his MP-5 onto his shoulder. He jumped down from the trail and gave chase toward the leading edge of the blaze. Cates watched him advance and then sped off to find away to get behind the glade.

Ellie was keeping to the thicket band that ran through the heart of the grasslands. There was no fire here yet, but wind carried gray smoke her way, and the fog bank style of cover concealed her well.

This stand of trees rimmed the cavern park grounds and was a veritable roadway straight to the equestrian facilities. She stayed low and paused shortly, just enough to check for signs of Porter.

She heard the motor just then and froze. She placed her back against a massive oak and peered around the trunk. There he was on the bike. He was watching the trees where she hid herself. He slowed and craned his neck all around to check for movement.

He traveled right past her. She shifted to her right to remain hidden and spared a glance to her left side. He peered in a moment longer and faced forward. She watched as he sped away.

She took a few quick deep breaths and tried to stave off hyperventilation. She groaned under the weight of her packs and stumbled away from the oak. She leaned forward to bear the load and get herself moving. It wasn't far now. She told herself she could rest when she was safely out of sight.

She turned her thoughts to Rain, she hoped that he was safe and would make it to the stables soon. The thought of a confrontation with Porter on her own did not appeal to her. For now, all she could do was keep her head down, and battle on.

Rain moved through drifting smoke barely visible, like a panther. in the night is slightly shinier than the darkness itself, barely a trace of him was seen. He emerged from the glade and straight ahead of him lay the blazing acre size stand of burning pines.

There was a branch of the horse trail here and he paused to check things out. He would have to wait here and he felt confident that he was well hidden in the dense undergrowth of the glade. He struggled to master his senses. His eyes and lungs burned but he made himself see and made his body breathe. He tried to get his ears to hear above his heart as it hammered away in his chest.

There it was. Not far off now. There was the sound of the dirt bike approaching his location. He peered out from the branches of the shrub trees and saw Dixon on the trail. He was armed and trained his gun side to side.

The weapon was still on his shoulder. It would take a second or two for him to bring it down and fire and that was all the time he would need to move when the timing was right. The rattle of the bike engine grew loud all of a sudden.

Rain grinded his teeth. The elements he was battling played tricks the whole time. He had misjudged now far away the bike was. Cates raced down the narrow trail toward his position.

Cates was coming fast and Rain knew it was now or never. In his distracted state of Cates' sooner that planned arrival, Rain hadn't realized he was a sitting duck. Dixon had unslung his machine gun and had taken aim. Dixon raced forward.

Rain ducked down as a burst of rounds turned the side of a oak by his head into a spray of heated wood chips. He shielded himself as a hole the size of a basketball was carved out of the tree around him. He glanced up and saw Cates standing on the peddles of the bike and the man sped closer.

It was now or never. Rain rushed from his cover and darted across the trail as a hale of bullets from both men tore trenches in the fiery ground right for him. Rain yelled defiantly and plunged himself headlong into the pines. The fire threatened to grab hold of him and eat him alive. He narrowly made it inside the hellish circle of their confines.

Cates slid the bike to a stop. Dixon came up beside him and they exchanged looks of disbelief. Cates scowled and pounded the bars of the bike with his fists.

"Fuck you, Ranger!" he yelled. "You lucky son of a bitch!"

"We're not goin in there?" asked Dixon. "Right?"

"We got no choice," said Cates. He stepped off the bike and appraised the situation. Dixon watched him intently. Cates pulled his coat up to cover his head the best he could and could still see Dixon from behind it's collar. He held his weapon in front of him and pointed the way with it.

Dixon nodded. He fumbled with his coat and managed to get it above his ears. He grasped his weapon firmly and prepared to run.

"Go!" yelled Dixon. Then he and Cates charged the inferno and punched through to the other side. Their coats yanked back down, they spotted Rain waiting for them at the center. He was backing slowly, farther in, and was drawing them with him.

"Hand over the bag, Ranger!" barked Cates. Rain continued backing away from him. Dixon advanced on him and thrust his weapon out at him.

"Hand it over now, or die!" he spat.

Cates fired a burst of rounds at Rain's feet. Rain danced backward. He checked around quickly. He was nearly out of the cluster and the soon the gunmen would be at the very center.

The trees were practicly alive. All around them, the trunks of pines heaved and shrunk back, as if they breathed the air. The skin of them underneath the bark bubbled and undulated. Rain saw this in his glance and he began to smirk.

"You want it?" he jested. "Come and get it!" He backed farther away and motioned to them to follow. "Come on!"

Cates took a step closer. A pine behind him cracked open and spewed a squelch of boiling sap with a loud "POP!" The liquid splashed down the back of Cates, burning him like a blow torch, and he screamed. Dixon jumped back and watched his partner flail as the sap ignited his clothes and he caught fire like a candle wick.

"What the hell?" he said. He turned his gun on Rain. Rain grinned at him and hit the deck. Dixon opened fire, yelling in anger and frustration, but only for an instant.

The blazing pines, their sap boiling from the inside out, exploded and a thick swarming cloud of the hot goo like a terrential rain, spread through the whole cluster from all sides and on enveloped the men.

Their screams pierced the air, louder than the forest blaze that roared all around them, as their flesh pitted, melted and began to drip from their bodies in heaps. They crumpled to the ground burning and dead.

The sap dissipated. Rain uncrossed his arms from his head and labored to his feet. The remains of the pine cluster lay smoldering, the trees reduced to strips of liquefying bark and wood. He ran across them, past the detritus of the bodies. Rain knew he had to reach the dirt bike. He had only seconds until the open area the blast created was gulped down the fiery throat of the mammoth blaze. It would seek to devour the fresh pocket of oxygen and he along with it.

Rain heaved the bike back upright and grabbed the pack of gold that lay near it. He whipped his head around and gave a startled gasp. He had heard the rumble amid the flames. He had to go now and go fast.

The rumble he heard, like a heavy thunder, meant the fire was going to roll it's molten wave of destruction over top of everything in it's path. Then a roaring filled his ears and he could see the hellish red cloud of pyroclest as it built to the breaking point.

He shouldered the pack with a mighty grunt and threw his leg over the bike. He stomped on the kick start and gunned the throttles to full. He flattened himself against the hot machine as it rocketed forward on the back wheel.

Rain could feel it tip further and further back as the weight of the gold threatened to drag him right off the back of the vehicle. He bore down, teeth clenched in a grimmace of determination, as he tried to force the front wheel down with all the strength he could muster. It worked.

The front wheel slammed onto the rough trail and bagan eating the dirt as the bike raced away. Rain was lit in an orange glow and glanced back.

The blaze surged into the clearing, like a tsunami gobbles coastline, and flooded the entire area with crazed fire. The flames searched out anything that wasn't yet ablaze and lit it up like kerosene. Rain locked his eyes dead ahead.

Rain roared out the fire as it rose behind him, his face a mask of desperation. He refused to look back at his destructor. If this fire was going to have him too it would have to chase him.

The bike gained speed to dangerous levels for such narrow passage and took to the wire grass fields. Rain's bike fishtailed but would not go down. He was free. The remnants of fire pawed after him and seethed in his wake like a pack of car chasing dogs that narrowly missed their intended prey.

CHAPTER 14

ROUGH RIDERS

Ellie got poised to break from cover. Her legs began to tremble as she held her crouched position and strained to listen for any movement or sound to tip her off as to Porter's location.

There was nothing. She couldn't hear the dirt bike. She cocked her ears right to left and could hear nothing in the woods that surrounded her. He wasn't in here with her. That was some measure of comfort.

She got on one knee, still poised to run when need be, and poked her head up from between the hanging limbs of two pine trees. She was staring at the front barn doors of the equestrian facility stables. She was less than two hundred yards away.

What if he was in there? What if he had his sights ready for her and gunned her down as she crossed? Where could he be? The questions swam through her mind one after the other about to drive her crazy, until finally, she gritted her teeth and charged into the open.

She was nearly dragged down by the weight of her rucksacks. She got her footing and forced herself forward. Quickly and quietly as she could muster, she crossed the open field, and flattened herself against the side wall of and old bunk house.

Ellie winced as a gust of super heated air rolled past her and she looked back to see that her wind break was now catching fire. Thick smoke began to churn up and clouded the open field.

"This is madness," she thought. They weren't going to make it. They had stayed just one step away from being swallowed up by the monstrous fire all the way, but now she was trapped. Porter would kill her here and take the gold from her, then it would be over.

She began to wonder about Rain. Had he gotten away, and if so was he on his way here? Could he get here in time? She shut her eyes tight and tried to focus her mind on the here and now and damn the what ifs.

Ellie jumped, and snapped her head around, alerted by the sound of the dirt bike motor off to her right. She watched and waited, hoping for Rain to come riding toward her, but it wasn't.

As the bike shot through an opening between two stands of flaming trees she saw the cold stare and confident smirk of Porter as he bore down on her and drew his weapon.

Ellie screamed, and flung herself away from the clapboard wall, as a burst of rounds from Porter shredded the corner where she had been into a cloud of smoking wood chips and dust. She nearly stumbled and continued to run, dragging a heavy rucksack behind her, she fought with it and got it upon her shoulder enough to run somewhat faster.

She rushed around the side end of the bunk house, skirted past a feeding trough, and charged for the double doorway of the stables. It was open and she could see the horses inside, grouped in the stables. She clenched her teeth and ran harder as she willed herself not to look back, even as she heard the dirt bike get louder as Porter came clear of the bunk house.

Ellie threw herself toward the open doors and landed in a roll amid the hey strewn opening. Porter let loose another burst of rounds that punched into the dirt and narrowly missed her legs and feet.

She shrugged off her last sack and with a grunt, slammed the big door shut on it's track, as a couple of more rounds drilled into the thick wood and knocked a plank loose.

All around her, spooked horses kicked and pounded at stall doors and walls with their hooves, and cried out to her with distressed whinny. Ellie got to her feet. They began to settle a bit in her presence. She walked down the rows of stalls.

Ellie opened a stall and approached a calmer horse. She held her hand up to him. He tipped his head up, wary, and surveyed her with a big brown eye down the length of his nose.

"It's okay, baby," she whispered. "It's all right."

She patted the nose of the horse and he began to settle quickly. He stepped closer to her and she rubbed at his neck, all the time she kept an eye on the barn door. She watched through the cracks in the wall as Porter stopped the bike near the troughs got off it, gun in hand. She continued to soothe the horse and when he nuzzled her hand with his nose, she knew he was safe.

Ellie gripped a saddle that hung on the far wall and side stepped him. She slung the saddle gently over him, and quickly and quietly, fastened it on, avoiding his nervous feet.

She ducked down. She watched under the stall gates as the door opened and Porter stepped inside. He looked all around. That supremely confident smirk made her blood boil every time she saw it.

"Come on, Ellie," he goaded. "It's over. I knew you're in here, so come on out."

He took a step farther in and jacked another fill clip into his gun. He swept the weapon left to right as he searched.

Rain pushed the dirt bike to it's limits. He drove hard, taking a curve that nearly dropped him, the bike and his body nearly straight out as it fought to stay on both wheels.

A wave of dirt, gravel and rocks was hurled in the air by the skidding machine as Rain held tight and stayed flattened against the bike as best he could.

The added weight of the rucksacks was all that kept the bike from whipping away from underneath him and it kept them on course. As the bike came out of the turn,

Rain sat up a little and heaved to his left, and forced the bike back upright.

Rain snarled as he focused his efforts to navigate the rugged terrain of the highland trails. He shot down into a rut between two jagged boulders that jutted from the earth.

If he had hit one of them, he would have broken off a wheel, and would have went flying to his death. The bike roared out from the rut and hit the top of the trail. Then it was airborne.

Rain held tight and gave a determined roar as he tried to stay on. He could feel his legs wanting to fly away and clenched the sides of the bike with both his thighs.

The bike came down hard and Rain grunted from the impact. He struggled to gain control as the bike fishtailed from the trail to the field grass and back again, whipsawing away on the verge of all control.

Rain got the bike aimed for the trail. His eyes widened as a tree loomed up ahead. He ducked down and shot underneath a low hanging limb and back onto the trail. His honed skills, almost instinctual in nature, was all that saved his head.

He let out a breath, a deep sigh of relief, and faced forward. He hoped Ellie would be all right. If she was at the stables, hopefully, she could hang on just a few more minutes and he would be there.

Porter moved slowly, step by step, down the center aisle of the stables. He did a double take as he noticed the horse at the farthest end with a saddle across it's back.

He grinned with malevolence. At last, after all this running, he finally had her pinned down.

Now he could have his vengeance for all the troublesome meddling, she and her forest ranger boyfriend had caused him. He would take his time with her, and then, the ranger would get his. His grin widened as he crept toward the stall.

"Yes," he began, "I would say there's nowhere left to go..."

He lept at the final stall. He reached over the gate and grabbed Ellie by a big handful of her hair. She screamed and slapped at both his hands as he dug in and lifted her off the ground.

He hauled her over the wall and stood her on her feet, face to face with himself.

"...accept straight to Hell," he finished. He took a step back, unshouldered the gun, and pointed it at her head. Ellie bit at the inside of her bottom lip as the tip of the weapon pressed hard against her head. She forced herself to stare Porter down as he prepared to pull the trigger.

"Go on, do it!" she snapped. "What are you waiting for?"

Porter seemed taken aback the slightest bit by her outburst. Then again, she was always too outspoken to suit him. He let his eyes wander over her a long time before gazing back into her eyes.

"I want to enjoy this," said Porter. "The least I can do is get a little fun of you after all the trouble you've caused."

Ellie sneered. It was almost as if she had channeled Rain through her and she even felt more defiant as she stepped toward him, forcing him back half a pace.

"I wouldn't touch you to scratch you," she said. She leaned in close to him and stared at him eye to eye. "So, it won't be so easy!" Porter shrugged and nodded in exagerrated agreeance.

"Duly noted," he said. He threw a back hand blow that slammed the gun against the side of her face. The metal opened up a gash along her temple and down her cheek.

She fell back against the stall walls and clung to the gate with her left hand. She wiped away her blood with her uniform sleeve as she struggled to get to her knees. Porter had begun to advance on her when the rattling motor of a dirt bike caught his attention.

He grinned down at her as he cocked his head sideways and listened. "They got him!" he shouted. "Looks like that's it for your ranger!"

He grabbed her by the hair once more and dragged her with him toward the door. She fought the whole way to get her feet under her. Porter kept ducking down to peer through the cracks in the walls and could only make out a single rider.

"So the ranger took another one out," thought Porter. No matter. It was all over with but the crying now. Soon they would be a lot richer than they were this morning and the farther away from here, the better. Porter slung open the heavy door and pulled her into the open. He waved to the rider with his gun hand.

"I got her!" he yelled. "I got-"

He saw that the rider was Rain. "Son of a bitch!" he growled, and started to take aim.

Ellie got one foot up high enough to kick him on the hip. He lost his grip on her and got forced out the doorway. Ellie fell to the floor. Porter glowered at her.

"Little bitch!" he snapped. He took his aim off Rain and pointed the gun at her. Then back at Rain as if unsure who was the greater threat. He settled on Rain.

Rain sped toward the barn. Porter turned the gun on him again and drew down a line of fire right at him. With a defiant roar, Rain turned the bike sideways into a slide.

Rain slid off and hit the ground hard. As Rain separated from the bike he planted his left foot hard on the seat and the kick gave the bike some extra speed and force going in. The bike skipped twice over the dirt, like a rock across water, and flew right at Porter. Porter's eyes grew wide as the bike roared toward him in the air.

"Shit!" he yelled. He dove to the ground as the bike sailed over him, and the back tire scraped the side of the interior wall, leaving a jagged burned gash where his head would have been.

Porter crashed into a barn support beam and lost his gun under the stalls. The bike crashed against the back wall of the stable and exploded.

Porter rolled out of the way, nearly unconscious from the concussion of the blast, as fire and debris fell around him. The impact had left a flaming hole in the side of the stable.

Ellie broke from cover and pulled her horse free of his stable. She snagged the bridle of another and hurried with them, past the prone body of Porter, and ran with the animals out into the yard. Rain ran to meet her.

"Are you okay?" he asked. He checked her over to make sure even as she nodded her head emphatically.

"I'm fine," she said. "Here." She handed off both the horses and started back to the stables Rain took a step that way.

"What are you doing?"

"Just a second."

Ellie ducked back inside. She searched around on the wall until she found what she wanted. There was a button to open all the stables. She had to let the horses go or they would be burned up.

She was about to slam her hand down on it when Porter suddenly lunged for her and grabbed her around the ankle. She yelped and yanked it away. She turned and planted her other foot, then delivered a thunderous kick to Porter's cheek, and the left side of his head.

He cried out and instinctively wrapped his head in his forearms, but he was out of it, and rolled over onto his back. Ellie made her way over to Rain as the first of the horses emerged from the barn.

Porter managed to roll himself clear, into a vacant stall, after getting stomped on the leg by an escaping horse. He crawled further in under the gate as the stampede swept past. Breath hissed from between his clenched teeth as he checked to make sure nothing was broken.

Rain was busy. He had the rucksacks slung over the back of one horse. Ellie quickly handed over hers and he added them on. The horses continued to jostle past each other into the open.

He got up onto the saddled horse and thrust out an arm for Ellie. She grabbed on and he heaved her up behind him. They watched the last of the horses escape and race toward the others that fled the approaching fire.

Ellie kissed Rain hard on the cheek and squeezed him around the chest. Rain squeezed her hands in return and smiled.

"Come on!" he said, and kicked the horse with his heels. The sleek black animal took off and was soon at full gallop, leading the other horse along.

They made it. Rain spared a glance back at the equestrian facility as the old bunk house began to catch fire. He nudged the horse again to spur him on and they gained speed across the open ground.

He glanced back once more at Ellie. She had her head buried against his back. He managed to plant a kiss on top of the crown of her head and turned around to focus on his ride.

The plan now was to make it to the Falling Waters side and call for help when they got there. They had a ways to cover and he hoped it wouldn't take too long. Porter was only down and not out, after all, and that meant he was still dangerous. Especially this close at hand.

His thoughts turned briefly to the hostages at the visitor center. Hopefully they were still okay and he hoped they could hang in there. He was convinced Tatum would do right by them.

Bradley and his team were driven back by the flames. One man caught fire and was quickly doused by his friends. Dugger frowned at them as they continued to battle. They were walled in. Just a handful of half dead men and women and a few vehicles that hadn't been destroyed were all that remained.

"What the fuck is taking so long?" shouted Bradley.

"I don't know!" Dugger yelled back. "Keep on fighting!"

Bradley's men were driven back again. He fell and one of his men tripped over him. Dugger broke from his line and left them to hold the hoses.

He dragged Bradley back and the fire threatened to consume them. The onslaught relented just in time as both men fell to the ground.

"Thanks,"panted Bradley. Dugger frowned at him. Bradley looked into his eyes. He was on the verge of tears.

"I hate this turned out so shitty," he sputtered. "For what it's worth, I'm sorry," Dugger nodded.

He was about to reply when over the sound of the roaring blaze, lame the undeniable rumble of engines. Not one dump plane, but two, were directly overhead. Dugger's radio crackled to life and the voice of Rick Conners, pilot of Red Bay One came over the wire.

"Brought a friend with us," he said. "Ready to get wet, guys?"

Dugger fumbled for the radio and brought it up to talk as he and Bradley helped each other to their feet. "Copy that," He returned. "Thanks a million!"

Dugger turned to face the rest of the brigade and motioned to hit the deck. "Everybody take cover!"

They scrambled away, dropped hoses, and sought the shelter of the nearest vehicles and ditches. As they were crawling beneath the trucks. Red Bay Two broke formation and headed toward them and the heart of the blaze.

The doors opened up under the plane as it dove toward the trees and a torrential wave of water, like the gates of a dam being opened, rushed out into the air and pummeled the blazing forest with hundred of thousands of gallons of water.

Once the water was unleashed on the flames and quenched the blackened landscape. Two jets of yellow flame retardant sprayed the area, and blanketed their vehicles under what appeared to be a thick coat of pollen.

Dugger and Bradley shared a look of terror mingled with relief and peered out from the cover of the water tanker they found. Smoke and steam filled the air.

Bradley got out with help form Dugger and looked around. For miles all there was was blackened earth and charred spears that once were mighty forest pines. All around, little crackles of flame popped and flashed and tried to ignite. Dugger turned to the rest of the crew.

"Let's keep the hoses going!" He bellowed. "We got it whipped now!"

He and Bradley manned a hose and smiled at each other as they saw Red Bay One fly off toward the cavern park. They did it. All they had to do was keep it damp and they would be okay. He said a quick silent prayer for the hostages a few miles away and opened the hose.

Tatum raised his head from the desk. His hair had left a puddle there from sweat. He could hear the sound of engines that carried on the roasted skies like rolling thunder. He allowed himself a hopeful smile. The plane. It had to be.

He scrambled from behind the counter, as sweltering tourists looked up, just now aware of the noise, Tatum made it to the window with Sue and Robbie on his heels. He threw open the blanket they had hung across the windows and could see the plane as it dropped out of the sky amid the smoke and fire.

Suddenly his vision was filled with an enormous tidal wall of white water as it instantly snuffed out the raging blaze and thundered through the air toward them, over them, and all around. He looked at the kids and then the others.

"Get down," he said. "Everybody get down!"

There were screams as the frightened people hugged each other and braced together. Tatum took the kids down and covered them.

The building shuddered and all the gift shop windows exploded as the impact of the water flattened burning trees and crushed the surroundings under the torrent of the water dumped from hundreds of feet above them.

Tatum rolled over. There was steam everywhere. The windows were gone and he could see the yellow retardant that covered everything like a thin scattering of snow flurries. He heard the engines rumble and drift farther away as the plane sought higher altitude.

The radio crackled. Tatum made his way between two clusters of people to get behind the counter. The voice of Conners was coming over the airwaves.

"That should just about do it," he entoned with confidence. "You guys all right down there?"

"Yeah," said Tatum. "Never better!"

He held the mike up as the tourists screamed and yelled their shouts of approval. Tatum put the mike to his ear so he could hear and Conners was chuckling a little.

"Good to hear it." said Conners. "We're off."

"Thanks," said Tatum. "Thank you so much."

He put the mike down and pounded the top of the counter with a clenched fist. The kids hugged him hard. They were crying and he cried along with them.

Porter staggered out the barn doors. He watched the two dots on the horizon that was all to be seen of Rain and Ellie. He fumbled with the radio on his belt. He changed the channel and brought it up to talk.

"You guys have company headed your way," he said. "Take care of it."

He turned the radio off and tucked it away. He glowered after Ellie and Rain as they rode out of sight. He heard the roar of engines and looked up to see the two dump planes soar past overhead.

He gritted his teeth. So the fires were out. He hoped they would be gone from here before that happened but that was fine. Once things start out shitty, they stay that way. You just have to try and salvage something from the day.

Rain glanced back. He reined his horse into a stop, turned sideways on the trail. Ellie shifted next to him to see as the planes came overhead. They watched them climb and circle back the way they came.

"At least everybody's safe!" exclaimed Ellie.

"Yeah," said Rain. "For now. Let's go!" He nudged the horse in the sides again and the animal took off at a trot. Rain snapped the reins and they were off to the races again.

The hostages were safe. So were the sweat hogs on the county lines. Tatum followed through. He was certain of it. He knew that the prickle of hairs on his neck meant Porter was still back there and would soon be on the hunt. But his nose was telling him danger lay ahead. He scowled and rode on.

CHAPTER 15

A GAME OF HUMAN CHESS

Porter struggled with his bike. He tried repeatedly to crank it up, but no matter how he worked at the throttles, there was no life for the engine. He tapped the gas gage, which read a hair less than half a tank, then decided to check it physically.

He twisted off the cap and peered inside. Sure enough, it was dry as the parched and blackened landscape that lay all around him. The woods of the wind break where he was were now fully ablaze. The dumpers had done nothing to quell the fire here, so he had to move fast.

The more he dicked around with this, the further Rain extended his lead. He knew he had back up waiting for them, but he wanted to be sure he was there to dispatch that Ranger himself. He had to get the bike going.

He got off and looked around. He spotted something around the side of the barns and shoved the empty bike in that direction. He coughed form the effort and from the thickening gray smoke. He made it around the side of the barn and yanked a tarpaulin off a shelf. Gas cans. Just as he thought. Now he was in business.

Porter unscrewed the lid to his tank and hoisted one of the red plastic containers off the shelf. He sloshed a good portion down the sides of the tank at first, but he finally got the can under control enough to fill his tank all the way.

He didn't bother with putting the can back where he found it. The way he figured it, the whole county was going up in flames, so a little spilled gas made no difference.

Porter tossed the can aside and the gas spread across the ground. He checked the fire. The old bunk house was catching now and would soon be ablaze. Time to go. He yanked the throttles and with a full tank of fuel the bike rumbled back to life.

He hunched himself down low against the frame and tore out from between the barns. He circled around and blasted out of the equestrian site in the direction Rain and Ellie had gone.

Rain and Ellie had covered a large amount of rough terrain in a fairly short amount of time. Thank God for the horses. Without them, he was sure they would have been caught by now. They still could be.

He knew Porter too well to think that he would blindly follow them, unless he had some sort of plan in place to make their capture easier. The man was cunning, everything about him was calculated and Rain knew that kept them firmly in his grip, no matter how big their lead was.

As they came around a dead fall and down onto a smoother section of ground that went out to a trail, Rain recognized the place, and knew they weren't far off from Falling Waters. They were just at the outskirts of the park grounds.

Now was as good a time as any to stop and let the horses take a breather. He could have a look around and get his bearings. See what was going on before they plunged headlong into an ambush. He held up his left hand so Ellie would see he intended to step, and began to rein his horse into a halt.

"What's going on?" asked Ellie. She made her horse come to a stop next to them, the pack animal grateful for the rest, nayed at her and quickly began eating grass.

"Just going to take a look around," said Rain. He got down off the horse and then helped her off as well. "Find out what we're in for."

"You think there's more of them?"

"Yeah. I'm sure Porter thought of everything."

Rain loosely tied the reins of his horse to the limb of a pine. Ellie tied the pack horse as well. She watched hm continue to munch on grass. There was no way he was going anywhere, but she thought you can't be too careful.

Rain followed the trail a short distance, staying on the balls of his feet, and kept low he made very little noise. Ellie kept right up with him and they came to a slight clearing that topped out on a crest that would make a decent look out point.

Rain gestured to hit the ground. He crouched down and dropped onto his stomach. He crawled forward on his arms and legs, like a soldier crawling through the mud. There was no barbed wire or grenades, though there might as well have been, as tightly coiled as his defenses had made him. He checked behind him and Ellie was struggling, but she kept up, and they came to rest at the top of the knoll.

Rain eased his head up to peek over the dome they were laying on and could just see the edge of the parking area for the Falling Waters Park and the entrance to the Sinkhole Trails. A man holding a gun came into view. Rain sneered.

He was right. He knew Porter. He glanced back at Ellie and tipped his chin up, urging her to take a look. She raised her head and caught a glimpse of the guman. She ducked back down just as the man started to turn in their direction.

"What do we do?" she asked.

"Let's fall back."

Rain belly crawled in reverse. Ellie watched him to see how and followed suit. They backed off from the hill and got to their feet at the bottom. Rain glanced behind them and took off for where they left the horses, his hand on Ellie's back to move her along, and she let him lead her.

They came to a stop by the horses. Rain checked over Ellie's shoulder again to see that they weren't heard or seen and had been followed. All was clear.

"If I distract them," he began, "can you make it on foot to hide the gold?"

"Yeah," she said. "But where?"

"I'll show you."

Rain got the horse free and Ellie untied the pack horse. He walked away in the direction they just came from and she pulled her horse along after him. They came back into the clearing by the old trail.

"On the other side of that hill," he said, and pointed to a rise in the distance. "You'll take the trail to a pond. Go around it on the left side and take the first trail you see."

Ellie nodded. Rain paused for a moment to listen and looked around them again. He leaned in closer to her this time and spoke again.

"There's an old oil well that's been capped off," he said, "been sealed for over thirty years. Dump the bags down the pipe and get outta there."

"I'll try," she said. He nodded to her and started to go. She grabbed him by the arm and he scowled, wondering what she wanted.

"The gold will be lost though." she said.

"I think they're too big to drop all the way," he said. "But you can pack them far enough down to hide them."

"Okay." she nodded. Rain made a movement to turn away and stopped. He turned to her and just watched her a moment. He smiled faintly. She was always amazing to him. Nothing ever changed that and he doubted anything ever could.

"You wanted to know why I came back?" he asked. Ellie nodded. "I never wanted to be in California. All I want is to be with you."

She reached up and cupped his cheek in her hand. She stroked his face gently with the tips of her fingers.

"I guess I forgot how to say it." he said. "How to show you." Tears leaked from the corners of her eyes and he reached out wipe them away with his thumbs.

"It's okay," she said. "Let's finish this and then we'll work on us."

Rain nodded. He took in a deep breath and seemed recharged by her assurance that all would be better in time. He was fortified and felt he could make it through. He was glad at that moment about all they had been through today. They needed the test, and they had passed it.

They separated. Reluctantly, they let go of each other's hand. Ellie moved forward along the trail with the pack horse. Rain stood there and watched her go. He alternately glanced from the hillside to her and back again, until she was gone from view. He glared, shark eyed and fierce once more, at the hillside and thought of the men that lay in wait beyond it.

That unnamed feeling was back. The thrill and stomach clenching sensation of coming conflict. A muscle twitched in his cheek as the determined tautness returned to his features. He tweaked on the anticipation of the fight for and instant and headed for it.

The gunman Rain and Ellie saw at the entrance to the trail was named Jacobs. He watched with growing bewilderment as a single saddled horse came walking toward him from across the parking lot.

He stepped cautiously out from his shaded cover amid the trees. He took out his baretta and looked all around for sign of movement. He didn't see anybody and gingerly approached the animal.

He softly touched the horse on the nose, then ran his hand down it's neck and rubbed there a moment, all the while he kept watch on the surroundings. There had to be a rider this animal belonged to out there somewhere.

Jacobs had no sense of being watched. But the horse without a rider was still disconcerting. He stepped away and let the horse meander about. He took his radio off his belt and brought it to his mouth.

"Porter," he called. "Porter, can you hear me?"

Porter was taking segments of trail where he could and taking the bike over rough and uneven terrain at others, but he was catching up. The woods had gotten thicker and it was hard going, but he was coming out of it.

He had just ridden down from around a dead fall when he got the call from Jacobs. He skidded to a stop at the continuation of the trail and listened.

"Porter," said Jacobs, "are you there?"

"Yeah!" snapped Porter. "What is it?"

God, how he hated dealing with these morons. This, he told himself, would be the last time he would do a job with hand picked monkeys like these. He was going to get fellow professionals next time. Men who knew how to handle things and didn't need to have their hands held. He waited with growing impatience for Jacobs reply.

"I have a horse with no rider."

This was beginning to be too much. He rubbed at his forehead with the back of his gloved hand to try and stop a building migraine. He believed they would ride headlong into the trap that he had set for them. What could they be up to?

"You're looking for two people," spat Porter, "and two horses!" He started the bike up again and prepared to leave. "Alert the others!" he snapped. "Spread out and find them. I'm nearly to you."

With that, he tucked the radio away, and shot off on the bike up the old trail.

Jacobs angrily sneered at the radio and turned on his heels to go back the way he came. He began walking back into thick woods of the trails on a large pine boardwalk system that traversed the entirety of the Sinkhole Trails. He was headed for the first of the holes.

"You got it!" he fired back. "I'm going to get them right n-"

He was cut off in mid sentence. A hand reached up from under the board walk and seized him by the ankle in an iron grip. He then got yanked off his feet and dragged underneath the railing by Rain.

Rain dragged the larger man through and he fell to the ground on his back with a resounding thud. Rain then made to dive on top of him but Jacobs caught him.

They rolled across the leaf strewn earth violently like an alligator in the throes of drowning it's prey, and Jacobs was able to kick Rain off him. The radio was left behind and you could hear Porter yelling out of it.

"What was that?" There was a long pause, then. "Jacobs!"

Rain was up first. He rolled from his back, up onto his knees, and into a coiled crouch. Jacobs staggered up and turned. Too late. Rain launched himself across the gap between them and slammed into Jacobs' chest with crossed arms in a kind of shoulder block maneuver.

"Jacobs!" cried Porter through the radio. "What the hell are you up to?"

Jacobs stumbled back over the lip of the sinkhole. He scrambled on all fours to try and stop himself from going down. He scrabbled and snatched at earth and rock and all the while the ground fell away under his boots and his hands found no purchase. He yelled in frustration and fear.

Rain stalked the top of the hole. As Jacobs moved around searching for a hold, Rain followed and stared him down, as if daring him to claw his way out.

His left foot crushed down on a jutting spear of rock and it gave way underneath his burly girth but not before he grabbed onto a vine with both hands.

He squealed and grunted disgustingly, like a rutting pig, as he franticly tried to haul himself up. He got one foot underneath himself and felt the thick vine get snatched taut, nearly yanked from his grasp.

He was precariously perched on the lip of the sinkhole. Below him lay flat sandstone boulders and jagged shale and limestone rock, every bit of sixty feet down. He looked up.

Rain glowered at him. He had the vine in one steely hand. With his other, he drew his knife from his sheath on his belt and notched it into the vine. He smirked as he looked from it to Jacobs.

"No!" Jacobs whispered excitedly. It was all he could muster. He was too frightened to do more than that. His voice had been taken away.

"Don't," he said. "Please."

Rain moved his hand, and with a slight twist of his wrist, the four inch razor sharp black blade sliced the vine in two. Jacobs instinctively grabbed it tighter and tried to pull it to him, but he was already falling backward. Already on his way down. He screamed all the way until a crunching impact cut him off.

Rain peered over the edge. Jacobs lay in a twisted heap, his body broken like twigs on the rock bottom of the hole. He lay across a big flat shale boulder splattered red with his blood.

"Jacobs," said Porter from the radio. "Quit screwing around and answer me!"

Rain straightened himself, walked over to where the radio was, and bent to pick it up. He brought it to his mouth and clicked the button down to talk.

"That's another one down," he entoned.

Porter had stopped the bike again to listen. Jacobs had said something else, but now he was not answering his call. He frowned deeply at the radio in his hand and was getting ready to hail him again, when Rain's taunt came to him.

He was nonplussed as usual. The fact that Rain and his girlfriend had reached the park so quickly didn't matter. He may not be able to close the noose around the ranger's neck, but perhaps, he could still choke the life out of him.

"You enjoy yourself killing my men," he barked. "I'll be there soon enough to finish all this business myself!"

"I'm looking forward to it," came Rain's reply.

Porter seethed. He made and angry hissing noise from between his teeth and clicked the radio to off.

The men would have to fend for themselves. Maybe the Ranger would kill them all and then he would have all the gold.

Porter smirked as he thought of that. Either way, at least he won't be hearing anymore chatter from them. "Have fun you son of a bitch."

He pursed his lips together in anger and gunned his bike to life. He took off, throwing up a rooster tail rut with his back tire, and drove like hell for the park.

Rain tossed the radio down the hole. He had no need for it. He had to be silent and he couldn't have it give away his position to any of Porter's remaining men.

He could hear them as they drew nearer to him. Their foot falls sounded hollow on the elevated walkways and the echoes of the movements carried on the still air. Rain stifled a cough from the smoke that still drifted on the wind.

"What was that?" he heard on of them shout.

"I don't know." came the reply. "I think it was Jacobs!"

Rain moved away, under the boards, and sat off toward them. It was the best cover he had, if he could stay under it a while more.

Rain looked around quickly. He spotted an area of the boardwalk up ahead that was over run with vines, wrapped around the banisters and railings. He scrambled over the uneven ground and narrowly avoided cutting his head on a protruding nail.

He grabbed hold of a vine and tested the thickness and the strength of it. Then he took two more in his hands and checked over them. He pulled these loose from the cluster they grew in, and began rolling them up.

All the while, he kept an ear open for any approach from the other men. He had to be quick.

He had very little time to work with, not only with the men closing in on him, but Porter was now more determined than ever to get here.

Ellie had followed the service trail that Rain pointed her to, and came out on a pine straw covered main trail to the recreational part of the Falling Waters Park.

She kept back in the trees until she could scout out the site. There were two men on patrol there, that walked around the side of the pond, where she had to get to.

The pond was full to the rim with a sandy beach and a swimming area blocked off by a heavy net from the rest of the water. The bulk of the pond was reserved for fishing and signs warning of alligators were posted all along the bank.

She crept out from the woods and led the horse behind a green building that was a changing area and restrooms for this part of the park and stayed close to the wall so she could peer out at them.

She scowled as some static crackled out of one of their radios and the sound of someone yelling was heard. She couldn't make out what was said, but whatever it was, it sent the two men running away from her in the other direction. They shouted out and drew guns as they ran into the woods. Rain must have created his diversion.

She waited a moment to see if they would return. Then she led the pack horse out around the corner of the building. They made their way quietly across the sand, past old grills and picnic tables, and came down by the edge of the water.

Ellie rounded the corner of the pond onto a trail that overlooked it and she led the horse along it until they reached the farthest end. She gave a sigh of relief as she spotted the trail that Rain told her about.

She stopped the horse and glanced around, back the way they came, and made sure no one was following them. She led the horse down the trail. Her heart was positively pounding. If Rain could keep them away a while longer it would be all right.

They made their way along it to a large pipe that jutted from the ground at the height of nearly two feet. The pipe end was capped by a metal banded lid. A small sign plaque marked it as an abandoned oil drilling site. She checked the rucksacks and thought it would be a tight fit, but it just might work.

Ellie tied the horse to a nearby tree limb and listened for a while for any sign of the men she saw. They were long gone and she knelt down to begin work on the band.

Ellie had no tools in her packs or anything she could use to pry the band loose from the lid. She looked around and spotted a few rocks that lay nearby. One of them looked to be big enough for her to hold in both hands.

She grabbed the rock and sat down on one knee at the front of the pipe. She hefted the rock, testing it's weight, and it felt heavy enough for a good makeshift hammer. She wet her lips, took in a deep breath, and prepared to batter the clasp of the band.

Rain waited. From his position, he had a good view of another gunman named Ortiz, as he came along the boardwalk toward him. He had to force himself to be patient. You had to have patience to catch a fish, and this was a lot like fishing. Ortiz just had to take the bait.

Ortiz moved slowly along the boardwalk. His eyes were wide and vered left and right. He crossed a section that traversed a natural bridge between two massive holes. He looked down into them off each side and glanced around again.

"Jacobs!" he called. "Where are you, man?"

Having heard no reply, he continued on, sweeping his weapon left to right. Rain continued to spy him as he came closer still. Soon he would be where he wanted him.

Ortiz reached the section of boardwalk where the vines had taken control. He continued to search the surroundings as he wove between the vines. He brushed aside one that hung curled up near his head.

The curled vine swung back toward him. At that instant, the loop dropped over his head and tightened around his throat. Ortiz dropped the weapon and it clattered away from him across the boards. He instinctively clutched at his throat and tried to loosen the vines grip.

The more Ortiz fought, the tighter the vine became, until his face was nearly purple from the pressure built up in his head. His body jerked and spasmed and still he slapped at the standing vine.

Rain had two vines in his hands and was pulling as hard as he could. He lay perched on a thick tree limb. He rolled himself off, on the same vine attached to Ortiz. He lowered himself down. As he came down, Ortiz was lifted off the platform, and the two of them came face to face.

Rain watched as Ortiz struggled for his last gasps of breath. Spit sprayed from the man's mouth as breath blew out and he groped at Rain. He was out of reach anyway. Ortiz's arms flailed at Rain one last time and his head lulled to the side, and he was gone.

Rain pulled on the vine and lowered himself the rest of the way to the ground using his full bodyweight. He held the vine with one hand for just a moment and his entire body shook with effort to hold the dead man in the air.

Rain looped the vine and around the trunk of the tree and crossed it over and under once. He let go of the vine and jumped back. The vine cinched tight and shaved a layer of bark off the trunk of the tree as it tightened up.

Rain breathed heavily, sweat beaded on his face, and he was red faced from the exertion. The kill had taken a lot out of him. He checked back over his shoulder and saw Ortiz hung above the boardwalk. The man's feet dangled about six feet off the boards.

Rain hitched in a breath. He could hear two others approaching him and glanced furtively around for a place to go. His only option was to try and make it to the natural bridge. If he could get there before they met up with him, he could get across to the other side of the trails. He headed that way.

Porter stopped his dirt bike at the point where the two trails divided. Despite everything, he had closed the gap in fairly short order. He now sat still and got a good look at the surroundings.

Up ahead of him was the dome shaped rise which Rain had used for his look out point not long ago. He looked the other way. This one was obviously some length, back way around the park.

He tried to think like the Ranger would. He would leave her with the gold sacks to hide, but he would also want to take care of her, to protect her while he dealt with the other men that were in place.

He leaned forward over the handle bar of the bike and surveyed the ground around him. It was then that he found the set of hoof prints leading away. There were two sets. The one going away plunged deeper into the ground as if it bore a sizable load. There were the faintest of footprints as well.

Now he knew. If he could get to the girl before the Ranger could save her, he could have his gold all to himself and her death would be a nice little capper for the whole mess, because he thought the Ranger wouldn't be able to live with that. He wouldn't be able to live with himself. That was the hero's lament.

Porter throttled up the bike and took off up the trail to his right. As he did so, he was glad he didn't have a conscience to get the better of him. Although they say everyone has one. If he did, at least his was such a squeaky mouse of a voice that he could choke it out without effort.

Ellie had been careful not to make much noise as she worked at getting the lid off the pipe. She would bring the rock up in both hands and sort of let it drop on the clasp that held the band.

She paused with her hands clasped around the rock. She could have sworn she had just heard the bike motor. She doubted Porter could have gotten here quite so fast, but decided she didn't want to greet him this way.

She threw all caution to the wind and banged the clasp with the rock. She drew back and slammed another hard blow and the metal piece bent down. It was severely weakened. She pursed her lips, raised the stone, and landed a hard blow that pitched her forward onto her elbows and sent the rock into the forest.

She glanced up. The clasp was broken off and nowhere to be-found. The metal band around the pipe was broken in two and hung there limply around it.

She paused to listen. She could still hear the faint ghostly sound on the wind that could be the bike. She wasn't sure yet, but she had to get this done. The gold wasn't his and she wasn't about to let him get out of here with it if she could help it.

She grabbed the band a little too quickly and gashed open the soft underside of one of her fingers. She drew back and looked at it. She sucked on the wound and spat it out. The metal was rusty and she had been quite awhile since her last tetnus shot.

She spat out her own blood and carefully removed the band from around the pipe. It wanted to coil up in her hands like an angry snake. She flung it away from her and it landed a few feet away in a pile of dried leaves.

She put her hands on the dirt and got her feet underneath her and stood. She went over to the pack horse and took off one of the heavy bags.

She dragged the rucksack over to the pipe. There was a lip where the lid was placed over the pipe and she got her toes under it and forced it off the pipe.

Ellie drug the bag a little closer to her and stooped to grab it. She hefted the sack in a bear hug and positioned it over the hole. She let go and the bag nearly caught on the lip. She gave a small shove and down it went. She watched it drop out of sight and could hear it sliding against the metal as it went.

She didn't hear it go down all the way, but it was in a pretty good distance. She was certain the others would all fit and be out of sight. Elle tore herself away from the hole and went back toward the horse to grab another rucksack.

Rain trembled with anticipation as he waited for the exact right moment to move. He saw Stork and Randall long before they made it to him. The old Natural Bridge was right in front of him and that was where he needed to go, but he had to wait. He forced himself to remain still awhile longer.

Stork had come around the boardwalk from an elevated section. This part gave tourists and up close look at the natural bridge between two of the deepest sinkholes in the state, if not the entire country. Each one was over a hundred feet deep and the old tree trunk that lay embedded between them was the only way across them.

Where Randall remained, the elevated boardwalk brought you around to look straight down over the holes. Rain watched from underneath his section as they a separated from each other.

Stork crept this way and pointed out Ortiz to his partner. Randall nodded and gave the hanging body a look of disgust. He moved behind a tree and came further around on the boardwalk to get a better view.

Stork watched him go, then crept forward, to where Ortiz hung above the boardwalk. As he went, he passed over top of Rain, who could be seen through the cracks between boards, if he had bothered to look down. Stork fought to control his bile as he took in the bloated purple face of Ortiz and the line of thick blood that had run out the side of his mouth.

"Oh, God," he breathed.

One of the vines that surrounded Ortiz's body moved from high up in the tree. Stork's eyes widened as he spotted the twitch of the vine and he jumped back.

"What's that?"

Stork sidestepped and raised his weapon. He opened fire at a limb overhead where the source of the movement was. A large gray squirrel sprang out from behind the tree limb and got clipped by a bullet. The animal fell at Stork's feet, where it writhed and squealed.

Stork walked up to it and fired another bullet that smashed into its head killing it instantly. Randall was directly across from him now. He chuckled at Stork's freak out over a little squirrel.

"All right," he jested. "Looks like you got the bastard."

"Screw you," Stork fired back. "The man that did this is here somewhere."

At that instant, Rain broke from cover under the boardwalk behind Stork and charged out onto the natural bridge.

Randall jumped in alarm. Suddenly, Rain was just there, right in front of him. He drew out his weapon and pointed at Rain as Stork whirled around to take aim as well.

"What the hell..." He squeezed his trigger but the clip was empty. He had to reload and began franticly searching himself for a full clip.

Randall fired into the air and Rain came to a sudden halt halfway out over the holes. Rain sneered up at him.

"Hold it!" commanded Randall. "Don't you move!"

Rain licked his lips. He glanced around furtively and knew there was nowhere to go. He turned his wide eyes back to Randall. The man just smiled as if he knew there was no way out.

Stork, meanwhile, had located a fresh clip and slammed it home in his weapon and he trained the gun on Rain as well. Randall glanced over at his partner.

"I got this" he said. "Keep looking out for those killer squirrels."

Rain inched backward as Randall mounted the railings of the boardwalk and prepared to jump. He wanted to come down and deal with him face to face apparently. That was fine by him. Rain welcomed the opportunity. He tensed up as Randall prepared himself and then lept from the railing.

Randall dropped down to land in front of Rain. His confidence soon turned to terror as he fell away right in front of him, dropping into the depths of the holes, where he screamed in rage as he fell.

Rain watched him pitch into the abyss. He had counted on this. What he knew, and what Randall didn't know, was that from above the holes on that side, the old natural bridge appeared to be intact.

In fact, the entire center of the old tree trunk that made the bridge had rotted away years ago, and it was the brackish brown sediment of the rock walls and the green moss that grew at the top of the holes that formed the optical illusion that made Randall think the bridge was whole.

Stork couldn't believe his eyes. He saw Randall make the leap and that he seemed fall through the bridge right in front of the man. He blinked stupidly a couple of times, forgetting the weapon in his hands, and that bought Rain some time.

Rain spared a glance back at Stork, then sprang forward and hurled himself across the gap in the old trunk. He landed on the other side and nearly lost his footing. He slipped on moss, regained control, and darted headlong across the remainder of the bridge.

Stork came back to the here and now, and remembered that he was in fact armed. He laid down a full clip of fire that chased Rain across the remaining distance. The bullets punched into the trunk, narrowly missing his heels, and threw chunks of dead wood into the air.

Stork grabbed onto a cluster of vines and prepared to climb over the railing and swing down so that he could give chase. He hauled himself awkwardly over the banisters and swung out on the vines.

The weight of supporting Ortiz's frame and the fact that the limb was mostly decimated by Stork's attempt to bring down the squirrel earlier, had severely weakened it. It gave way and dropped Stork unceremoniously on his feet.

He lost the weapon as he roughly landed and he pitched sideways. He got his footing and looked up to see what the problem was. There was nowhere for him to go.

The massive limb slammed into him head on, knocking him off his feet, and crushing most of the bones in his entire body. He couldn't even yell. He was dead before his feet left the ground.

The limb swung backward and deposited Stork's broken body on it's belly and then whipsawed around on the leaf covered ground before coming to a stop.

Rain watched the aftermath from across the gap and scrambled away again. He was certain that was the last of them. He had to find Ellie and get away from here before Porter could get to her. He hoped that she was at least able to dispose of all the gold. That way, Porter had nothing to gain anymore. And yet, nothing to lose.

That thought chilled Rain to his very bones. He shivered and though his body ran at a fever pitch, as he sweated and grunted his way through the underbrush. He shut his eyes tight for a moment to force the thought back into hiding. He opened them again and he battled on.

Ellie had forgotten her task for the time being. She had been listening intently ever since the first volley of gunfire moments ago and waited with baited breath for any sign or sound of Rain.

She hadn't even realized that for the last few moments that she was no longer alone. Porter had crept on the bike up to her location and now waited with that cheshire cat smile close behind her.

Ellie forced herself back into action. She wanted to know what was going on and how Rain faired, but she still had some work left to do. She turned to go to the horse where the last bag sat on the ground she hefted it, still unaware that Porter was behind her, and prepared to turn to the pipe and drop it in. He clicked off the safety to his weapon and she jumped and cried out.

"I wouldn't do that," said Porter, "If I were you."

He tipped the barrel of the gun toward the ground a couple of times, urging her to put it down, and she dejectedly let it slide out of her arms and crash to the ground. He let his eyes wander over her for a moment and his evil grin broadened.

"What a day- what a day!" he exclaimed. "You know, there's still enough gold in that one sack to make us both very rich."

Ellie looked at him with disgust. She hated his looks, the sight of him, the smell even. All around, he was repulsive to her, and certainly at no time was her dislike made worse that when he made these advances toward her.

"I like your spirit," he said. "I'm sure you could be quite good with that attitude, if directed under the right hands."

"Go to hell!" she yelled. "Take your precious gold and leave us all alone!"

Porter was about to respond when the last burst of gunfire rang out in the distance. Ellie jumped and Porter took his gaze from her to look in that direction.

Porter had leveled his gun at her just before the shots were fired. She saw the look in his eyes and knew he intended to kill her for spurning him again and have the gold as well. She had to make her move, now or never.

She bent and grabbed the heavy sack. She rushed toward him a couple of steps just to get some force built up. Porter turned to her but it was too late to avoid what happened after.

She heaved the rucksack at him. Porter caught the bag. It slammed into his midsection and knocked him backward. He fell to the ground with it on top of him.

"You fucking bitch!" He swore vehemently. He rolled the bag off himself and sat up. He grabbed the weapon off the ground and brought up the gun to take aim. Ellie dove toward the woods and, the sharp drop off beyond the oil well pipe as Porter opened fire at her.

The bullets ripped tree limbs and leaves to shreds as Ellie dove clear. She dropped over the edge amid the cloud of debris and Porter got to his feet. He ran to the edge of the trees and peered over the edge of the drop. Dirt was being thrown up by her rapid descent and there was no way to stop her now. Porter turned away from the edge and left her to fall.

CHAPTER 16

END OF THE LINE

Rain had made his way onto a section of boardwalk that led toward the falls that gave this side of the park it's name. He moved cautiously, yet it would be easier to make up time on the boards, now that he didn't have to duck and dart over the uneven ground anymore.

He couldn't get over his luck so far. He knew the land well. Better than anyone else had, and he had pushed himself beyond what he thought his physical limits were, to get the job done.

He had to find Ellie and end this now. If he could keep moving, maybe he wouldn't be too late. Porter was close by. He had to have reached the trail that led here by this time. He forced himself to move a little faster.

Rain was watching for any sign of other gunmen when he was stopped in his tracks by a barrage of gunfire, from high up above his position. He sat there frozen and stared up at the edge of the trees where he thought the shots had come from.

His eyes widened in terror as he saw Ellie crash through the limbs and undergrowth and go over the drop off. She slid down the side of the hill and tumbled faster still, toward him. Rain caught a glimpse of Porter as he peered down. He tensed but Porter didn't see him. He turned his attention back to Ellie.

She rolled over a small cluster of brush trees and turned into a feet first slide. She was headed underneath the boardwalk and the last of the large sinkholes was just a few feet beyond it on Rain's right side. He saw she was turned to go right at it.

"Ellie, no!" he yelled.

He tried to anticipate where she was going to go under and dove for what he hoped was close enough for where she would punch through. He slung out his right arm and waved it back and forth. He kept the faith that she would spot him and make a grab for him.

She did. Ellie slid underneath the boards, her arms over her face. She caught a brief glimpse of Rain's meaty forearm as he waved it around. She locked on with both hands, slid down his arm taking off sleeve with it, and gripped his hand in one of hers.

It was enough to slow her momentum tremendously but she couldn't hold on. She had pulled him halfway underneath the railing and their hands broke free of each other. She screamed in frustration.

"Ellie!" yelled Rain.

He tried to lunge and reach her again but she slid past. She dug her heels in and begain to slow herself down and clawed at the ground as she slowed her descent. She came to a stop at the very edge of the hole.

Rain was on his belly, his forearms under his chest, tensed in anticipation of what would happen. Ellie looked around herself and gave a little jump, frightened by seeing into the depths of the sink.

"Ellie," he began. "Just don't move."

"Okay," she squealed. "I just don't like heights."

"I know, honey." said Rain. "Just a second and let me think."

Rain looked her over. She couldn't use her feet to push herself from the edge. There was no way to get a foot hold. The ground was fragile there and would give way underneath her.

There was a root system of a massive oak was exposed to the elements just to her right. If she could grab onto that, she might be able to haul herself away from the danger zone.

"Ellie," he began. "I need you to lean to the right. There's a bunch of tree roots there. You need to grab one."

"Okay," she said. "I'll try."

Ellie leaned to the side and tried to grab the nearest root. She narrowly missed. She kicked her leg out in her attempt and the soft ground gave way underneath and left her foot to dangle there. She nearly panicked when she didn't feel it there anymore and she squealed again.

"It's okay," said Rain. "You're all right. Try it again."

She pursed her lips together, determined, and leaned to the right. She lunged with all the strength she could muster and grabbed onto a thick exposed root with both hands.

With a straining grunt, she used her arms to pull herself back three feet from the edge of the sink hole. She lay there and panted. Rain watched her until she got her breathing under control.

"I'm coming to help," he said. Rain made a move to swing his legs under the boardwalk rails. Ellie held up her hand to stop him and wave him off.

"I'm okay now," she said. "I can make it back up." She raised her eyes toward the top of the cliff face that she slid down. "Porter's got the rest of the gold and he's going to get away if you don't stop him!"

Porter hissed through his teeth. The nerve of the bitch tour guide. He wished he had just went ahead and put a bullet in her when he first rode up behind her. It would have been a lot less aggrevation.

At least she was out of the equasion for now. He doubted he would have anymore problems out of her but it was the Ranger he worried about. He was still out there hunting and he knew he didn't have a lot of time here.

All through the course of this day, Porter longed for the chance to meet the man who had caused his so much trouble, and to squish the fly in his ointment. But now that he had the gold in his posession, he just wanted to ride on out of here and be done.

He went over to the bike and heaved it back onto two wheels and let the stand down. He hefted the rucksack that she had thrown at him and layed it across the rack at the back of the seat.

Just to make sure he didn't leave it to chance that the rest of the gold was lost, he went to the pipe and peered inside. He saw nothing but blackness. He knelt down and put his arm in up to the shoulder and grabbed around inside.

There was nothing to be had. Still, he considered himself better off than he had been. He still had a quarter of the fortune he started out with and that quarter was worth nearly four hundred million dollars at today exchange rates.

He smiled about this. He may have taken some damage, suffered some losses, but had he really lost? He didn't think so. His smile broadened as he walked over to the bike, got on, and started it up.

Rain whipped his head around and glared up at the top of the tree line. He could hear the bike motor as Porter reved it up to cut out of here.

"Go!" exclaimed Ellie. "I'll be fine!"

Rain nodded. He charged up the steps to the next section of boardwalk. He rounded the corner banister and followed it along the rim of the canopy, up more steps, grunting with effort to force his legs to churn and churn to get him higher.

He glanced to his left and could just see the top of the waterfall in the distance that this part of the park was named after. It's whitewater erupted over the cliffside and he could hear the rush as it cascaded downward. The sound of it was powerful even at this distance away.

He looked to his left, and could see Porter coming closer on the dirt bike, through the tree line. Rain charged hard up the last flight of steps as Porter's bike rocketed past, buffeting him with hot air. Rain shielded his eyes with a forearm from the flying grit thrown off by the tires.

Rain took the last two steps in a single bound and tore himself out from behind the railings and onto a natural trail along the top of the park. He was right among the canopy of all the trees that grew down below near the sinkholes.

Rain was running full out. His lungs burned and hurt from the effort to keep up his pace over the uneven ground. He leaped over logs, boulders and jumped to avoid the tangles of tree roots that threatened to take his feet right out from under him.

Up ahead of them both stood a wooden bridge that traversed the expanse of the whitewater and connected the trails. Rain ran harder and felt on the verge of blackout to try and get there. He knew that if Porter crossed the bridge and made it onto the wire grass trails, he could ride to the parking area, and then he would be gone.

Rain clawed thorns out of his path and now flanked Porter on his right side. Porter spotted him moving through the trees and did a take as he checked ahead.

"Come on, asshole!" yelled Porter.

Porter made the bike turn, prepared to cross the bridge, and put his head down. He gave the throtle another half twist and the bike rocketed forward onto the boards.

Rain dug in hard as he plowed along the river bank and charged toward a jumping off point where the hill crested up ahead of him. The bike was already near the middle and he didn't know if he could made it, but it was his last effort.

With a defiant yell, Rain leaped from the bank. His foot had planted squarely on the rise and propelled him into the air. His legs drove hard and pushed him across the gap,yelling all the way.

"Yaaa-ah-ah!"

Porter heard the determined scream. He turned half way around on the bike and brought up his gun. He fired off the full clip of rounds and one of them hit Rain in the left shoulder.

Rain's body got spun halfway around in midair, but he was still able to hook his right arm around Porter's midsection and rip him from the bike.

The bike crashed head on into the support beam at he end of the bridge and exploded. Rain and Porter, locked firmly together, fell through the side railings amid the fireball and black smoke. They crashed into the icy water below and were plunged underneath.

Porter struggled to get up and fell again. The current of the water was far stronger than he expected as he and Rain washed underneath the bridge. Now both men struggled to get their footing.

Porter was the first one up. He charged in and launched an awkward, yet still powerful, kick at Rain. His momentum was thrown off by the water speed and strength. Rain tried to block with both hands but the boot connected, and slammed him square in the chest.

"Ughh!" grunted Rain. He sputtered and gasped just to breath. Rain went down with a tremendous splash. He rolled himself away, letting the current work for him as he continued to gasp for air, and swallowed a big gulp of cold water. He could see that Porter had gotten his legs under him and he advanced on Rain.

"Get up!" he barked.

Rain was up. He got his footing and tried to charge. Porter was ready for him though and threw a thunderous right hook that pounded Rain in the head. The mighty blow snapped his head back and he was nearly out on his feet.

Both men went down from the force of Porter throwing the punch. Porter was right back up though and sloshed toward Rain, who had begun to drift farther down stream. Rain struggled in the rapids and was finally able to get to one knee.

He couldn't help but marvel at how relentless the man was. Every bit as icy as these rapids and he was determined to do him in at all costs. That much was abundantly clear. Porter was nearly on him again.

"I said get your ass up!"

Porter grabbed Rain by the collar and dragged him around in the water. He was either going to be drowned or beaten to death by the water. Every single wave that rolled over him pounded his aching body like a boxer. Porter continued to drag him while he held his head under.

Rain dug his feet into the river bed to stop the dragging and threw an uppercut that blasted into Porter's gut. With no fat on him for protection to soften the impact, it was agonizing. Porter instantly let go and doubled over, coughing and gasping for air.

Rain stumbled up to his feet. He planted himself and charged at Porter. Rain slipped on a rock in the river bed and landed in an awkward head down lunge, that hit Porter low, tackling him around the waist. They tumbled into the water and rolled over four times.

Rain cursed his luck. Just when he could have gotten some momentum on his side, he had to hit that rock. At least Porter was getting a good taste of what if felt like to get rolled over by this water. He was going to have to make a shift in the power struggle happen before too long, or it would be the end of him.

Both men came up gasping and coughing. Porter seemed to have the harder time of it. It was now or never. Rain staggered toward Porter and slammed a right cross into Porter's head. Porter cried out in mingled surprise and pain. He fell hard into the water again.

The splash the man's body made hit Rain in the face. He stumbled back, wiping at his eyes. He was able to clear his vision enough to see most of what was going on around him. Porter was already up again.

Porter struggled to gain balance and did so. Rain came rushing in on him and threw another right hook. Porter was able to block. He grabbed Rain's right arm and held it against his side. He then punched Rain three times on the leaking wounds in his shoulder. A fresh flow of blood erupted from underneath the blow.

"Ah-ahhh!" screamed Rain. "God damn!"

Rain dropped down on his knees, teeth clenched in agony, nearly passed out from the sheer ferocity of the attack and the unbelievable throbs of pain that coursed through him. It was as if Porter continued to pound the wound repeatedly.

Porter still had Rain's arm pinned by his ribcage. Porter measured him a moment and then lifted his left knee. The heavy blow smashed Rain across the face and slashed him open above the eye. Rain fellback ward in a spray of water and his own blood.

Before, they only just flickered, threating to extinguish. This time the lights that were on in his head went completely out. The power of the blow was astounding He couldn't believe how much strength Porter still had at his disposal.

The cold of the water and the exhaustion of trying to remain standing and trade punches was getting to be too much. He let himself go with the disconnected feeling he had right now and shut his eyes.

Just as he was about to give into the darkness that wanted to consume him and take him away, there was his old familiar friend, pain. The rapids rolled him and pounded him and gave him fresh soreness as he drifted. He was coming back around thanks to their unyielding beat down.

The river was merciless. An unstoppable force of nature. Yet, Rain was surviving all it could throw at him. If he can survive the river's might, then Porter he decided, was no big trick. His anger and determination blazed anew, and he struggled up, waist deep in the middle of the rapids.

He started to go down again as Porter charged him. He blinked away the rest of the cobwebs and got his wits about him just in time to slip under Porter's wild hey maker of a left handed punch and grabbed him around the waist with both arms.

Rain cinched his arms tight and thrust Porter back against his chest. He leaned in close to Porter's left ear and growled, "My turn."

Rain hefted Porter out of the water, and hurled him bodily, belly first back into the water. Porter got rolled over a couple of times, thrashed by the waves, and came up hacking. He struggled to draw any breath at all. It was like getting slammed on concrete.

He stumbled backward. Rain was advancing on him with a snarl spread across his face. For the first time, Porter saw what it must have been like for the rest of his men, as this rabid dog bore down on him.

Rain launched himself at Porter and drove his right forearm into his chest so hard Porter felt like his body was going to collapse in on itself. Both men were once more taken off their feet and thrown to the mercy of the river.

Rain swam over Porter and used his upper body weight to hold him under. He looked up and did a take. The edge of the falls bubbled up dead ahead and the current was faster as it drew them on toward the edge. Both men pulled each other up, gasping, and struggled to stay above water.

Rain's attention was caught by movement on the river bank. Ellie had arrived at the edge of the water. She had a large limb that she thrust out into the raging torrent and tried to reach it out for Rain to grab onto.

He couldn't believe her. Her determination to see this through was every bit as strong as his. No matter what, she couldn't be kept down. That tenacity was another of the things he loved so much about her. Still so funny how you can forget.

"Grab on!" she shouted. "Grab on, I'll pull you out!"

Rain struggled to reach out for the tip of the limb. He made several swipes at it as he fought to hold his ground with the push and pull of the river so strong against his legs.

He had just clenched four fingers around the end, as Ellie strained to hold the limb out as far as she dared, when Porter grabbed him in an iron grip.

"No you don't," snarled Porter, and dragged Rain toward the falls. "You're coming with me!"

Ellie dropped the limb. There was no way she could reach Rain now. She got up and ran along the bank to follow them. They were battling each other as well as the current.

Ellie watched them from the edge of the bank. She was nearly in the water herself and she cried out as they drifted to the very precipice of the falls.

"No!" she screamed. "Don't do it!"

Porter stopped them. He was braced against Rain and Rain was braced against him. They looked like two wrestlers when they locked up at the start of a match to feel each other out for weaknesses.

Porter tried to punch Rain one last time and missed wildly. Rain drew back as far as he could and head butted Porter on the nose. There was an audible crunch when it broke. Porter cried out as blood gushed from his crushed nose.

Porter staggered, and cradled his nose in his hands, as blood soaked the front of him. Rain tried to turn and battle his way back from the falls. Porter lashed out and wrapped his arms around him. They were locked together in an embrace as if they were long lost brothers and then over the edge they went.

This was one of those times when a split second seemed to take an eternity to pass. They had slipped on the rocks at the edge of the falls and had been driven out into thin air. They seemed to be suspended, just the slightest of moments over the hundred and seventy- five foot drop.

Rain and Porter tumbled down about forty feet to the overlook platform that tourists use to get a close up look at the falls. Rain managed to separate himself from Porter's clutches enough to turn, and reached out for the railings, and grabbed hold.

The platform positively quaked under the weight of their impact and railings snapped like dry kindling. The entire rail section nearly ripped from their moorings from the force generated by both screaming men as they tried to stop their plunge toward certain death.

Rain hoped against all hope that the timbers would finally shore themselves up at one of the stronger joints and stop their descent. He didn't come this far and put himself through this kind of hell today, just so he could fall to a watery grave with a murdering theif.

At last, the banisters stopped pulling away from the base of the platform, though they still groaned in protest. Rain allowed himself to relax his mind sightly and felt it might actually hold them until he could figure a way out of the predicament they were in.

Rain grunted with effort, muscles straining, to keep his grip on the busted railing. Up above them, Ellie had caught up to them as they struggled. She reached out to him, a reflex gesture that could do nothing, but it still gave him a little comfort as if she willed nothing to happen to him.

"Hang on!" she pleaded. "I'm coming for you!"

The railing groaned again and he heard a snap. Rain took his eyes off her long enough to see another of the boards was pulling free of it's nails. He shot a quick glance back up at her.

"Hurry!" he shouted back.

Rain yelled in agony as Porter grabbed onto his wounded left shoulder to pull himself up.

Rain clenched his teeth and growled behind them as Porter's fingers clamped down over the wound.

"Too little, too late, Ranger!"

He dug his fingers into Rain's wound again. Rain screamed out in sheer agony as unbelievable pain washed over him.

"Yaarghh!" he screamed out.

Rain let go with his left arm and they dropped another few feet as the railings snapped loose once again. Rain yelled in pain as he hooked his right arm around another part of the railing to keep them hanging on.

Ellie cried out again when they fell. She had intended to leave but she stood transfixed by what was happening with the two men. She finally made herself move and she began making her way down the side of the hills that surrounded the lookout area.

Porter was cackling like a hyena, crazed fury in his eyes, as he pulled at Rain, his body bucking as he tried with all he could muster to pry them both free from the railing. Rain wriggled his upper body free of Porter's grasp. Porter glared up at him.

"We go together, Ranger."

"Fuck you!"

Rain elbowed Porter repeatedly in the face with his bad arm and cried out in fresh pain each time he forced himself to pummel the man. Porter yelled and was forced to let go. He slid down to Rain's waist, lost his grip there and then slid down to cling onto one leg.

Rain's body trembled in every muscle fiber as he struggled to keep the both of them hanging on. Everything he had was focused on not letting go no matter what. The voice in his head cried out for Ellie to hurry, to just get here already, and he hoped she could somehow pickup on what was going through his mind.

Porter tugged furiously on Rain's leg. Up above them, the platform gave a shudder and then they were met with a loud creaking sound as more nails in the railing threatened to give way Porter's grip tightened yet again and he redoubled his efforts to break Rain's grip.

"You're going with me!" yelled Porter.

Rain tried to turn and bring his foot up. He aimed a kick that hit Porter in the side of the head. He kicked at him again and again, and succeeded in nailing Porter right in his fractured nose.

Rain heard the sickening squelch as his boot came down on the damaged tissue. That would have to do it. There was no way Porter could take that and continue to hold on. He heard him cry out in pain and instantly felt the strain and pressure on his lower extremities release. He was loose.

Porter let go, arms flailing and yelled, as he realized he had no hold on Rain and that he was falling away.

He continued to scream in terror as he plummeted the remaining hundred and thirty feet to the bottom of the falls.

"Ah-ahah-ah!" he yelled, all the way down. Then the scream was abruptly cut off by a heavy thud, nearly drowned out by the pound of falling water, that came to Rain's ears. He didn't want to look, but he had to see for himself to know, and glanced down.

Gray shale rock had been painted dark red and the pool below began rapidly turning crimson as the blood of Porter's broken body mixed with the crashing water from the falls.

It was over. Thank God. He hung there just a moment longer and closed his eyes. He tried to clear his head so he could focus on what he had to do.

The platform railing wasn't going to last much longer. Even without Porter's additional weight to hold, it still creaked, popped and trembled to even hold Rain any longer. He had to move or he was going to join Porter after all.

Rain began dragging himself up. It was an arduous task, in his condition, to say the least. He kept an eye on the few nails that were left to hold the railing. He reached up and cautiously pulled himself to another section of falling rail.

So far, so good. It was slow going. He crept with his movements slow and deliberate and tried no the exert anymore pressure than the crippled structure could stand. To do so took an enormous toll on his body.

He paused where he was as a full body shudder wracked his beaten frame. The vibrations were so strong he feared they might weaken his grip until he fell. His muscles simply wanted to shut down now. He willed himself to reach out and grab another timber and haul himself closer to the top.

Ellie had made her way down the steep and unstable hillside, careful foot hold after careful foot hold, until she made it onto the boardwalks. She climbed over the banister rail and started down the flight of steps that took her to the section that dropped down to where the overlook platform was. She came off the last step and headed that way. As she went she silently prayed for Rain to make it. To not give up.

Rain labored to reach for the top of the platform. His palm slid off the slick surface and his nails dug trenches in the dampened wood. He tried again and failed, tried again, and finally got a hand hold on the end of the two by six planks.

He kept his feet planted on the railing by the tips of his toes. He winced as he raised his left arm and tried to get it under his chest. He glanced up and could see Ellie on the boardwalk. She was nearly to him.

"Tom!" she called. She was crying and waved to him as she came down the last stairs to the platform. He nodded to her and gave a grunt for a reply as he tried to do a kind of push up to raise his torso up against the platform.

He hitched in breath,out of surprise and pain, when his left arm gave out, and the limb simply folded up underneath him. He was falling and kicked out with his feet. They found the railing, but the impact was too much for it to handle.

He couldn't hold himself up this way with only one good arm and the piece of railing faltering below. Ellie threw herself to the timbers of the platform and slid on her stomach to him. She whipped her arms out and locked onto his good forearm.

He pushed off the platform rails again and hoped it would hold just one more time for him as he pushed up his body weight with the one arm. He pushed and Ellie had turned sideways where she lay from pulling so hard.

The last nail ripped from the platform base with a loud squeak just as Rain gave a defiant yell and heaved himself up onto the lookout platform. He rolled over onto his side next to Ellie and panted with exhaustion.

The railing swung off from the platfom and fell away to the depths of the falls. Rainstruggled to control his rapid breathing as he realized how narrow his escape really was.

A lock of his black hair obscured his vision but he turned his head to the right. Ellie was sitting up and was watching over him. He managed to half way smile at her. She wiped the hair out of his eyes.

"Are you all right?" he asked.

Ellie's eyes filled up with tears and some leaked out and ran down her cheeks, leaving trails on her skin, as they washed off dirt and smoke. She laughed a little. Rain smiled more. He liked hearing the laugh. It was starting to make him feel among the living again. She shook her head at him.

"You're asking me that question?"

Rain sat up and laughed. She laughed with him just a second, then got up with her hands on her knees. Rain got a knee up, reached out and took her hands with his good one, and she helped pull him to his feet.

Ellie let loose with a coughing fit as she helped him up the stairs and off the lookout platform. He held onto her when they went up to the landing and watched with concern until she stopped hacking.

He glanced around. He hadn't paid attention to it before, but the smoke had gotten thicker.

Perhaps the dump planes weren't able to put it all out. They weren't in any immediate danger, he didn't think, but when you've been in it all day the smoke just got to be too much after a while. She glanced up and saw the concern etched on his face.

"It's okay," she said. "Smoke's finally getting to me. I'll be fine though."

She grabbed onto his waist for him to lean against her so she could help him along the boardwalk. He saw nothing but a steady uphill climb and more steps ahead of him. He simply waved her off and leaned his back up against the banister.

He was too tired to take another step, much less deal with more stairs. He just wanted to rest and relax a little and be with her for now. They finally had a quiet moment today and he wanted to hang onto it. She let him slump back and she propped herself up across from him. Rain sighed.

"I don't think I can move a muscle." said Rain. "You don't mind, do you?"

"Not at all," she said. "It's fine with me. Whatever you want to do."

She smiled. Truly smiled. The warmth and caring contained in that single expression touched him in ways it hadn't touched him for a long time now. He pushed himself off the banister and hobbled a couple of steps toward her.

"This is what I want to do." he said, then he leaned in close to her, cradled her cheek in his good hand, and kissed her deeply for a few moments. He stepped back and she caressed his jawline.

They both looked up at the sound of sirens approaching from the distance. They were getting there fast too. They took a few steps in that direction and heard the patrol cars as they came to a stop in the parking area, not far from there.

They saws the first of the green clad state troopers enter the woods on the boardwalk. Tatum was behind them. They heard his voice before they saw him. He was calling out to them.

"Tom!" he cried. "Ellie! Where are you guys?"

"Down here!" yelled Rain.

Tatum edged past the Troopers who had stopped to marvel at the dead body of Ortiz that hung over one of the sections of boardwalk. He ran toward them and came to a stop just a couple of feet shy of them. He glanced back and forth from Rain to Ellie a couple of times, trying to figure out where to start.

"Everybody's okay," he began. "The dumpers got to the park just in time."

"That's good." said Ellie weakly.

"I met up with those guys." said Tatum and indicated the troopers with a backward glance.

"Got here as soon as we could."

Rain hated this. He absolutely hated the way things had turned out. He never in a million years expected anything could happen to cause such an awkwardness between him and his best friend.

The day's events seemed to have far reaching consequences. It will take years for the land to get back to normal and hide the damage done by the fire, and it was going to take even longer for Tatum to make amends for his part in the crimes.

Out of a need to make some quick money to ease a great financial burden, Tatum had started a fire that destroyed the forest and indirectly led to the deaths of several innocent people.

Tatum seemed to have picked up on what was going through Rain's mind because he forced himself to meet their gaze.

"It's taken care of," he said. Rain and Ellie shared a curious glance and Tatum dipped his head down to avoid seeing it. "I told them everything."

Ellie looked directly at him. Her hatred of him had dulled to pure bafflement at how he could have done the things he had done to help Porter and his men. She also felt sorry for him now and the look she gave that conveyed that emotion was hardest off all to take. He gave into tears.

"I'm so sorry about everything that's happened." he said. "Whatever they do with me, I deserve it, and more."

Rain tried not to break down. He felt Tatum's pain and knew he really meant what he said. His jaw twitched as he fought not to cry for him. He reached out and clapped him on the upper part of his arm.

"Maybe it won't be too bad." said Rain. "Remember you did bad things, but you also did a lot of good for a lot of people in the end."

"That should count for something." added Ellie. Tatum merely nodded and was able to meet their eyes again.

One of the Troopers came over and stood next to Tatum. He was obviously waiting for him. Tatum glanced back at the man and turned back to Ellie and Rain with a crooked smile.

"I guess it's time for me to go."

He smiled at them one last time and turned to the Trooper. He held out his hands and Rain frowned deeply as he watched the handcuffs get clamped on his friend's wrists. The trooper began to lead Tatum away.

"Good luck," called Rain. Tatum half way glanced back at him. He simply nodded and let himself be led away. Ellie wrapped her arms around Rain and held onto him as he watched Tatum go. She looked up at him and saw the sadness there.

"You gonna be all right?" she asked.

"Yeah." he said and looked down at her for a moment. He kissed her on the forehead and held her close to his chest with his good arm. Now he knew the hero's lament. You couldn't save everyone, no matter how hard you try.

AUTHOR'S NOTE

Dear Reader,

What a ride, huh? I hope you enjoyed reading this as much as I enjoyed writing it. The idea for it sort of came through word of mouth over the years. Rumors and tales of buried Indian gold flare up every now and then around my area, particularly in the places I used for the setting of the Marietta Cavern Park in this novel. Whether those stories are true or not, I thought they would make for an action packed adventure, and I used them as the catalyst to create one.

For the location in the novel, I combined two different state parks near my home, into one, to serve the needs of the story better. The real parks I chose to use are the Marianna Caverns in Marianna, Florida and Falling Waters State Park in Chipley, Florida. They are actually about thirty miles from each other, but

I always thought that combined, they would make the perfect backdrop for my novel.

The first time I ever went to these parks was on school field trips and I have been back many more times since then, and still continue to go back. The wonders of nature never get old, and these are two of the most beautiful places to go, to see nature up close.

So, if you're ever traveling through Florida, I urge you to visit the Marianna Caverns and Falling Waters parks. Who knows? Maybe they will somehow inspire you as they have inspired me. At the very least, they should provide you with a good place to rest, and get some fresh air, and take in some gorgeous scenery. Until next time, take care.

Yours,
Charles